BIGGER ▧▧▧▧▧▧ 'N ▧▧▧▧▧▧ DALLAS

BIGGER 'N DALLAS

KURT TIDMORE

GROVE WEIDENFELD   NEW YORK

Copyright © 1991 by Kurt Tidmore

All rights reserved.

No part of this book may be reproduced, stored in a retrieval system, or transmitted in any form, by any means, including mechanical, electronic, photocopying, recording, or otherwise, without prior written permission of the publisher.

Published by Grove Weidenfeld
A division of Grove Press, Inc.
841 Broadway
New York, NY 10003-4793

Published in Canada by General Publishing Company, Ltd.

Library of Congress Cataloging-in-Publication Data

Tidmore, Kurt, 1950–
Bigger 'N Dallas / Kurt Tidmore. — 1st ed.
p.   cm.
ISBN 0-8021-1393-1 (acid-free paper) : $17.95
I. Title.
PS3570.I28B5   1991
813'.54—dc20   90-28900
                                CIP

Manufactured in the United States of America

Printed on acid-free paper

Designed by Helene Berinsky

First Edition 1991

1 3 5 7 9 10 8 6 4 2

For R. O'C.

Not a stone, not a bit of rising ground, not a tree, not a shrub, nor anything to go by. . . .

—Francisco Coronado, Spanish explorer
of the *Llano Estacado*, 1541

Llano Estacado, *or* Staked Plain: *extensive tablelands . . . destitute of both wood and water.*

—S. Augustus, cartographer, 1872

Tyrone County sits in the southern part of the Llano Estacado *(Spanish for Staked Plain) surrounded by and encompassing some of the finest, flattest irrigated farmland in the state of Texas. The county seat, Tyrone, has a population of almost 2,000 friendly people and provides three churches, a supermarket, a modern cotton gin, and all the other amenities for modern living.*

—from pamphlet entitled *This Is Tyrone!*
published by the Chamber of Commerce,
Jerry Wintergarten, President, 1972

1

Steven Paul "Spud" Merton

Spud Merton followed the last of his employees to the door, then opened the wall panel and switched off the big neon sign in the parking lot. The yard-high letters spelling out BIGGER 'N DALLAS quit their nervous flickering and went dark, leaving the night sky unbroken. He stepped outside and locked the door.

"Night, Spud," the barmaid said as she got into her boyfriend's pickup.

"Night, Mary Lou."

The idling pickup revved to life, opened its brilliant eyes, and charged to the edge of the parking lot, rattling gravel under its fenders. In a moment it was only two red taillights moving away in the dark.

Spud walked to his station wagon, carrying his car keys and money bag in one hand and his pistol in the other. One night many years earlier he'd run into trouble after locking up. It'd cost him three hundred dollars and twenty stitches in his scalp. Since then he'd always carried a loaded pistol when he left. He'd only needed it one time, when a couple of hopped-up cotton gin workers tried to jump him in the dark.

But he always carried it. He didn't even notice it anymore, no more than he did his car keys.

Spud hadn't been married long when that first robbery happened, and his wife had gotten very upset about it, sure it would happen again, only worse next time. She'd tried to talk him into selling the bar and put a lot of energy into making up violent scenarios in which he was attacked by hoodlums, robbed, and left for dead; blood in the moonlight and nobody knowing about it till it was too late. But he wouldn't sell. And she'd seemed almost disappointed when, night after night, he'd failed to live up to her anxieties.

Spud had no interest in getting a day job. Running that bar, working from five or six in the evening till two in the morning, was the only thing he knew that would let him pursue his real passion, which was catfish. It was probably this as much as fear for his safety that had upset Ethel. To her way of looking at things, going fishing every night wasn't normal. Spud had pointed out that it was mentioned in the Bible (he'd looked this up), and he'd quoted the line from the gospel of Matthew where it said "Go thou to the sea, and cast a hook, and take up the fish. . . ." But this had only made her tighten her mouth into that expression he'd always hated.

At first he hadn't understood her opposition to his fishing. It wasn't as if he were neglecting her or having an affair with another woman. But the fact was, he wouldn't have traded those hours by the pond for an affair with Miss America, and it finally dawned on him that that was why his wife hated it so much: fishing was a rival she couldn't compete with. The night he realized this, the moon had risen late, shaped like an eye, and sat on the horizon watching him as he baited his hooks and put out his lines. He caught four big ones by its silvery light, and this pleased him more than anything else on this earth could have. As he took in the fish he decided that nothing but death would ever make him give up his "going down to the sea, and casting a hook, and taking up the fish," even though his sea was only a little round pond on the prairie.

Spud had begun night fishing when he was still single, back during the Depression. Prohibition had ended and he'd opened the bar, but times were still tough and meat was expensive. Fishing was a way to help make ends meet. The pond was on old man Tarbuckle's land; he was a regular customer back then and had given Spud permission to fish whenever he wanted. Over the years he took a lot of catfish out of the pond, using a homemade stink bait he concocted of blood and cornmeal. At first it had been strange to go fishing at that time of night—he seldom got to the pond before 3 A.M.—but the fishing was good because catfish are night creatures, and after a while he came to enjoy the quiet dark too. He learned to identify the night birds by their songs and taught himself the names of the stars from a book someone had left in the bar.

When times got better and Bigger 'n Dallas was more successful, he didn't need the fish for food anymore, but his enjoyment of the night and the solitude kept him going. He'd stay at the pond till the rising sun pinked the sky, then pack up his rods and his folding chair and go home and cook himself some bacon and eggs and fall into bed just as Ethel was getting up.

Things had been hard between him and Ethel almost from the beginning. After a few years it was as if they'd divorced and divided the universe in half in a kind of cosmic property settlement—she had the daylight hours and he had the dark. But sometimes in winter she'd already be up when he came in and he'd have to share the breakfast table with her. When this happened, they'd look at each other with sullen resentment, as if each were infringing on the other's terrain.

As often happens, they'd married with completely different ideas about the arrangement. He thought she'd stay the same, and she thought he'd change. He was tough and big and secretive and wild, and she saw him as a romantic character. She was sure that beneath his rough exterior there was a heart of gold, just like in the stories she read every month in *Reader's Digest*. When they first married, she'd waited for the heart of gold to shine through. But it never did. It remained as hidden as if it did not exist at all, as if his insides were as cool and dark as an unused closet. She had hoped he would be someone she could depend on and discovered only too late that he was; he was as dependable as nightfall. He would keep on being just what he'd always been.

For his part, Spud had seen Ethel as a spirited, slim-waisted, smiling girl, and he'd expected her to stay that way forever, unchanging as a taxidermied fish, reliable as a good hospitalization policy. But she could no more stay that way than the moon could stay put in the sky. So the two of them had been bound for disappointment from the very beginning, and it wasn't long before they discovered it for themselves. After twenty-five years of marriage, all he'd noticed about her was how the lines around her mouth had deepened and set so that her lips looked as if she'd closed them with a drawstring, and all she'd noticed about him was how his belly had annexed the airspace over his belt buckle and how the veins in his nose had plotted a road map across it. Both of them had felt cheated. Gypped.

Ethel died sitting in the middle of the congregation of the First Baptist Church at a Sunday service just before the plate was passed. Brother Kinder had been tying up the loose metaphors in a sermon about how Jesus recruited Simon and Andrew and James and John, how He'd promised to make them "fishers of men," and how they'd thrown down their nets and followed Him, leaving behind their families and businesses and everything. Maybe Ethel was thinking about her husband at home snoring away after spending all night catching catfish, thinking that she wished Jesus had picked a better class of people to start His church with. Or maybe she was suddenly infuriated that Spud wouldn't throw down his fishing tackle and take up a reformed life, like the apostles had. Or maybe she was thinking something else entirely. But whatever was on her mind, she seemed suddenly overtaken with rage and stood up as if she was going to interrupt the sermon. Brother Kinder looked down from the pulpit and saw her, and he hesitated between two words, caught mid-metaphor by the expression on her face. For an instant she just stood there with her mouth open, as if she would shout some invective or some accusation, then she pitched forward like a felled tree, landing on top of Mrs. Wild, who was sitting in the pew in front of her dozing and oblivious to what was happening. Both of them ended up on the floor. It was not like a story from *Reader's Digest*.

They'd tried to telephone Spud from the church office, but he'd taken the phone off the hook. So finally one of the deacons drove over and gave him the news. The deacon, an old man and a widower himself, sat there at the kitchen table with his hat in his hand, ready to give comfort. But it wasn't even noon yet and Spud was having a hard time getting his bearings, much less showing sorrow he didn't really feel. Finally the deacon left, saying Spud could call him and talk if he wanted to, he knew how it was.

A few nights later, when the funeral was past, when Spud had gone fishing again and was sitting in his usual spot smoking his pipe, staring at the net of reflections the breeze had cast across the water, a kind of hollow feeling came up in him like a bubble. For the first time he noticed the barrenness of the plains spread out all around, and loneliness seemed to form on him like frost.

After that, the bar and the pond became his whole world. In the darkness of the bar, which he expanded with Ethel's life-insurance money, he poured beer and hired bands and kept order among his customers. In the darkness of the pond he sat in his folding chair and watched his rods, stiff against the water's shimmer. And wherever he was he thought about catfish, implacable and alien, citizens of a city of mud, living their lives in an atmosphere as dense as the smokiest bar in the world in the middle of the darkest night. He didn't like the light himself, and realized now he never had, so if forced to go outside while the sun was up, he took to wearing the darkest sunglasses he could find. Eventually his eyes became wide and black and glassy like portholes in a sunken ship, and children began to make up stories about him, and dogs that were friendly with everyone else cowered back and barked when he passed.

The smoke from his pipe drifted away in little puffs, rising at a forty-five-degree angle like spooks ascending in the moonlight. It was five o'clock in the morning. The sun was still an hour beyond the horizon. The bass and crappie were sleeping in the inky calmness of the pond. Only the catfish were feeding. It had been a slow night so far, but Spud had been through a thousand slow nights. He puffed his pipe, leaned back in his folding chair, and glanced at the tips of his rods. Down below, the catfish were sliding smoothly through the dark, conversing with one another about the quality of tonight's stink bait like gourmets in a restaurant, twitching their mandarin whiskers. An hour earlier a six-pounder had tried its luck. One of the rods had jerked twice and pointed itself at a spot in the pond like a divining rod reaching for water. Spud had jumped up from his chair and taken the rod from its holder and started hauling line, reeling in the fish, calculating its length and weight before it ever came into sight. Catfish don't jump. They stay to the bottom, always pulling down, hoping to wrap the line around a submerged stump or a junked washing machine or a big gob of weed. When they're finally brought up, they cut the water with their dorsal fins like sharks, fighting the line with the power of their tails and carving big, quick esses. That six-pounder was tethered to the bank now by a metal chain clipped through one gill. The others were still conferring.

Lately there'd been fewer fish, and practically no small ones. So far tonight, nothing but this loner. Spud thought about this: it's spring. The water is just starting to warm. They ought to be hungry now, especially the little ones. Maybe somebody's fishing in the daytime. Maybe something's gotten in the water. Maybe I'm finally fishing the pond out. He turned these thoughts over slowly in his mind like a man examining a strange coin that's come to him in change. All these years he'd fished this pond, studied the ways of catfish, meditated on their whims and moods, but they were still a question without an answer.

Just then the tip of one rod began to bend very slowly. Spud stared at it, sighting up from it to one of the small stars of Perseus lying on the horizon. It *was* bending. He stood up and stepped over to where the rod stuck up in its holder. The line led tightly from the old bait-casting reel up through the guides to the tip, then straight as a draftsman's line to a point in the darkness where it met the water. Beyond that, somewhere, it ended in a hook and a fish. He strained his eyes but couldn't see where it entered the water. It was moving too slowly to cause a ripple.

He stooped and took the rod from its holder, and with a "hep!" he reared back against it and set the hook. But it was as if he had baited his line with a can of Quaker State and cast it into the bar's parking lot and now some big, thirsty Cadillac had taken it and was heading for the highway. The fish just kept moving away, paying no attention to him whatsoever. He seemed to be having no more effect than if he'd snagged a submarine. He held the line as tight as he could and out of habit started doing his mental calculations as to the size of his opponent. By the time the fish finally turned and started back toward him, he realized he'd hooked something that ran right off the scale, and as it approached, an image sprang to mind of a drunk who'd walked out of the bar one night and stood in the middle of the road waiting to punch an oncoming semi in the nose. He backed away from the water, pulling line as he went. The fish kept coming. Thirty feet from the bank, it made a wide turn and started away again. Spud clamped his hands on to the rod and held on. This time he thought there might be some reaction, but the fish kept going, staying at the edge of the weeds that fringed that side of the pond, pulling him slowly toward the water until the soles of his boots squished in the mud and he either had to let out line or get ready to swim. His hands slackened slightly. The fish took the line it wanted. Spud only tried to rein it in a little, as if it were a horse.

He'll get tired eventually, he thought as the line scraped through the guides, tight as a guitar string. Won't take long for him to get his fill of pulling against me. He's just a fish, for Christ's sake. Spud imagined himself dragging the fish up on the mud, then hauling it back to town lashed to the roof of his station wagon like a canoe. Probably find old tackle boxes and outboard motors in its stomach.

The fish made a turn at the end of its run, and at the end of that run it turned again, and then again. It moved slowly but continuously, taking line and giving it up, taking and giving up.... As night revolved slowly toward day the invisible fish circled and pulled against Spud and against all the years he'd spent beside the pond. It pulled him till his hands felt locked to the rod, till his arms trembled and his back ached. Behind him, in the east, the sky began to define itself from the earth in a gradient of slowly brightening gray. The first redwing blackbird called from the cattails, a bullfrog on the far bank began to *ba-room, ba-room* in its bass voice. In the pearly light the place where the moving line entered the silver plane of the water became visible, and Spud followed the path of the fish around his mental map of the pond's bottom—the deep hole where the spring entered, the place where the willow roots sank their knotty fingers in the mud, the margin of floating moss.... Around and around the fish circled as if looking for an exit. But there was no exit. There was only an old man waiting on the bank with mud on his boots and impatience growing in his stomach like an appetite. And the fish was beginning to slow, yielding to the constant pull. Finally there was a slight roll on the water at the far end of the turn.

"Easy now," Spud said under his breath when he saw it. "Eeeeeeasy."

And the fish headed toward him, rising as it came. Spud hauled line, keeping the hook tight, until the fish began to show itself.

First there was the dorsal, then the long smooth back, then the wide flat head, the beady black eyes, the gills dilating slowly just below the surface.... In the slanty dawn light the fish seemed to have an expression of total disgust and revulsion. Spud had never thought about a fish's expression before, and he was as startled by this look as by its gigantic size. He hesitated for a moment, and as soon as he did the line slackened and the fish turned against it and broke it with a dull twang. Then, slowly, the monster sank down out of sight, the broken line dangling from its lip like a strand of spaghetti.

For a second Spud stared at it, unable to believe what had happened. Then he dropped his rod and ran to the car and threw the door open and grabbed the revolver and pointed it. But the pond was as smooth as a pane of glass. There was only the sound of the bullfrog. He walked back down to the water's edge. "Damn ... damn ... damn," he muttered, searching the pond with his eyes. Nothing.

Finally he snorted and stuck the gun in his belt and began to take in the rods, glancing occasionally at the spot where he'd last seen the fish as if it might look out at him again like a face in a window. But it didn't. He snatched up his chair and carried it and the rods back to the car and threw them in with an angry clatter, hoping something would break.

At the edge of the mud the six-pounder was patiently fanning its pectoral fins. Spud stood over it and watched for a moment, then stooped and carefully removed the clip from its gill. The fish stayed where it was until he poked it with his finger. Then, almost reluctantly, it swam away.

On the way home he listened to the radio—Kansas City hog prices, the forecast for spring cotton, commercials for John Deere tractors and the Future Farmers of America and Purina Pig Chow. On his street the paperboy was pedaling along the sidewalk, flinging newspapers across the empty lawns at one closed door after another like an athlete practicing for some obscure sport. The boy turned and stared as he drove past. Spud glared back from behind his dark glasses.

In the kitchen he ate in silence. Then he went to bed.

Sometime in the late morning, for no reason, he opened his eyes. Through the closed and darkened window he could hear the sounds of daytime; a car drove past with its radio on, a door slammed somewhere down the street, the branches of a honey locust scratched softly at the corner of the roof like the fingers of a man scratching the ear of his dog. From the edge of the closed blind a thin white line of sunlight reached into the room, stretching itself across the rug, over the toe of a boot, up the front of the dresser, and ending there beside a paperback, its pages curled like flower petals, and an old oval wedding photograph in a silver frame. The gleam on the frame was the curve of a hook hanging into the darkness of the room. Shapes moved in the shadows. Up above, barely visible beyond the mirror of the water's surface, someone was waiting, sitting in a folding chair.

⌦⌦ 2 ⌫⌫

Billy Bumpus

Under a sky full of stars, Billy Bumpus pushes his rig along the road that leads through Brownfield, Gomez, Tokio, Plains, Bronco, Tatum, and on toward Roswell, heading west, eventually for California. He's left late to avoid the weigh station at the New Mexico line—it closes down about ten-thirty—so now it's pitch-dark and he's cruising down the highway, listening to the radio and practicing that peculiar kind of high-plains meditation brought on by the combination of no turns, no hills, no traffic, and an endless series of white dashes unrolling in the headlights. Every so often he goes through a little crossroads town all shut down for the night except for maybe a 7-Eleven manned by a sleepy local kid with bad skin and no prospects. But these are the only breaks in Billy's white-line meditation, the only places where he comes up for air and sees what's around him. If he were viewed from above, say, from that airplane the Department of Public Safety keeps threatening to use to catch speeders, his truck would appear as a small dark rectangle lighted at each end, playing a giant game of connect-the-dots with the little patches of brightness these towns make on the otherwise unbroken surface of the prairie. But nothing could ever be high enough to see what symbol he might be tracing out. Billy Bumpus will go on connecting one town to another in a more or less straight line until he hits the western escarpment of the plains just outside Roswell and starts the climb up into the Sacramento Mountains. He'll have to downshift to get up that. And there will be turns.

But until he gets there, he's just staring at the unwinding white dashes and listening, through the road noise, the wind noise, and the low rumble of the old diesel engine, to the crackly radio signal of station WOGR (the call letters, he is told, stand for Word O' God Radio) as it comes down to him from the heavens via the marvel of atmospheric skip from its broadcasting tower way up in Scottsbluff, Nebraska. The voice he hears is that of someone called Brother Ray Bob, Evangelist of the Nation's Highways, Every Trucker's Copilot and Every Gear-Jammer's Buddy. Through the static, he is delivering a sermon in a voice that sounds like sand running down a metal chute or like a crosscut saw. He says:

"Ya know, my gear-jammin' buddies, when you're high-ballin' it down that looong looonesome road o' life, you want a road map. Somethin' to SHOW you the WAY. Point out the BAAAD stretches, the closed bridges, the ripped-up pavement, the gravel two-lanes with chug-holes big enough to lose a K-Whopper and a load o' cattle in, the waiting weeeiiiigh stations, the radar traps hidin' behind the Lucky Strike billboards. You wouldn't THINK of haulin' a load ANYWHERE without a map, would ya? And when you pull into a truck stop for that midnight cup of coffee, why, what's the first thing you talk to the other truckers about? It's the road ahead, ain't it?! A man wants to KNOW where he's going. CERTAINTY, great Jesus, THAT'S what you want, idn' it!? CERTAINTY THAT YOU'RE GONNA GET WHERE YOU STARTED OUT FOR! You ask about the road ahead and some good ol' boy travelin' the other way asks about the road behind. 'Now, Brother, you better watch out around that Chi-town,' you say, ' 'cause there's construction on the eastbound. Better be careful goin' over that hiiiigh mountain pass, my friend, 'cause there's ice on the turns.' Warnings! WATCH OUT! TAKE CARE! I BEEN THERE! I *KNOW*!! And you and your buddy remember these things so you won't be caught wantin' when the time comes. And then you drink your coffee together and you eat your chicken-fried steaks, and when you're through eatin', and after you've checked the oil and whacked the tires and tanked 'er up, you hit the road again, confident you can handle what's comin'. Confident because you're expectin' it. My buddy told me, you think. And maybe you mark these things on your map so's to watch out for 'em.

"Well, brother truckers, the problem with life is that there ain't NOBODY goin' the other way. I'm here to tell you that we're ALL HEADED INTO ETERNITY TOGETHER!!! You CAIN'T stop off at a Little America along the way and get advice from some good ol' boy who's been there. Because EVERYBODY is HEADED for the DAY OF RECKONING TOGETHER! It's a ONE-WAY STREET, and there ain't NOBODY gonna be comin' back sayin', 'Now you watch out, Brother Ray Bob, for that temptation that's a-comin' up when you get to be forty. Be careful now. Don't you fall for that little truck-stop cutie you're gonna meet when you're forty-five. She's a SPEED TRAP laid for you by the PRINCE O' DARKNESS! Don't you go beatin' on your kids any more'n's good for 'em, now. The LORD has GOT YOU IN HIS SIGHTS from that TRACKER PLANE in the SKY.' No, sir, there AIN'T any sort of warnin' on the highway o' life, my gear-crashin' friends. Everybody THINKS they know. . . . They THINK the road ahead is clear all the way to the other side. But the fact is, we're ALL headin' into EEETERNAL DARKNESS with our HEADLIGHTS OFF!!! And SOONER OR LATER we're AAALLLLLLL gonna come up on that sign every trucker dreads!

DEEEETOOOUUUURRRR. *DETOUR!!!!* Great GOD, it strikes fear in the heart of every long-haulin', fast-drivin', gear-crashin' man in America!! Detour! It means slow goin' and busted-up pavement and low bridges and long waits and heavy traffic and windin', twisty roads that seem to take you farther and farther away from where you wanted to go. But there just ain't no way around it. When GOD ALMIGHTY puts a DETOUR on the ROAD O' YOUR LIFE, you got to TAKE it. There'll be temptation lyin' like busted bottles on the shoulder. There'll be WRONG TURNS at every intersection. Toll booths, weigh stations, oil slicks, watered gas . . ." (And here the signal from WOGR, only an atmospheric fluke all along, begins to break up and lose itself in Mexican polka-band music from someplace south of the Rio Grande, so that Brother Ray Bob comes in only in occasional hoarse shouts over the blaring trumpets and thumping drums, like a man yelling across a crowded dance floor.) "HOW DOES A MAN . . . WHAT TO DO?!?! Well, tru . . . map . . . can talk to . . . what you've got . . . one person . . . JEEEEEEEEESUS!!"

Billy knows what Brother Ray Bob is saying without having to hear all the words. He's heard it a million times before. Ever since he was a little boy and used to go to the Miracle Tent Revival Meetings with his Aunt Fay and stand in the dust and the stuffy smell of strangers, watching the Jesus man sweat dark arcs under the arms of his coat and cut the air with sharp gestures like he was boxing with ghosts until finally a woman (his wife?) would start playing "Just as I Am" on a big black-and-chrome accordion with a blood-red bellows, squeezing out the asthmatic notes to accompany her thin, reedy voice. "*Ju-ust as I a-am, withou-ut one pleeeaa . . .*" she'd sing, and the preacher, hoarse from breathing the dust and exhausted from boxing with the ghosts, would speak the same words and ask people to come forward and meet their savior. When Billy tried to keep himself awake on long dull stretches of highway, he'd sing the hymns he remembered from back then, wailing them out the open windows of his truck into the empty night. They were better songs for singing than the Top 40. They seemed to suit his voice, and their refrains about salvation and sacrifice made more sense on the dark highways. *"On a hilllll far awayyyy, stands an ollld rugged crooooss, the syyyymbol of suuff'rin' and shaaaame . . . ,"* he'd sing, fighting to keep his eyes open and the truck from slipping off the road, fighting with the murderous unseen forces that wanted to kill him, just like the preacher boxing with the ghosts. *". . . and exchaaange it some daaaay for a crownnnnnnn,"* he'd howl over the wind noise.

'Course he never did this when he had somebody in the cab with him, a hippie hitchhiker or something. Then he'd listen to KOMA from Oklahoma City just like everybody else, listening to all the announcements of upcoming concerts: "Spider and the Crabs will be at the Armory in Garden City on the eleventh," the deejay would say in that fast talk they always talked, "and then at the town hall in Hays on the fourteenth. The Executioners are coming up at the American Legion post in Coffeyville on the tenth. Rosco and the Rockets will be at the Oil Well in Bartlesville tomorrow night, and . . ." They played rock and roll and a few country-western songs and a whole lot of advertisements and announcements. Or maybe instead of KOMA, they'd listen to the ballroom-dance music from "high atop the Roosevelt Hotel, deep in the heart of old New Orleans," as the announcer always said, rolling out the words in a voice as mellow as a slide trombone. Anything but the screamers, the sky pilots, the radio preachers with their talk of eternal damnation and sin. It was only when Billy was alone that he tuned around his dial searching for these God-crazed voices of doom to keep him company.

It was almost as if there were two Billys living in the same skin—the Billy who drove long stretches singing hymns until he was as hoarse as Brother Ray Bob, and the Billy who got out of the truck in some little town and went to the first bar he could find to get drunk, dance up a storm, and pick up as many willing women as he could find. Two separate lives. Two separate histories.

The hymn-singing Billy was the nephew of a woman named Fay McCool who prayed over her food till it was barely warm, and never left church but when they turned the lights off, and saw visions, and heard voices, and was acquainted with the Devil in all his forms, and knew the words of all the verses of all the hymns that'd ever been written. Aunt Fay had raised this Billy from the time his parents—her sister and the man she'd married—died when he was five, up until he ran off at the age of sixteen. She never married, and Billy was the only man in her life besides Jesus, Who she treated as an invisible inhabitant of her little house. His picture hung in every room but the bathroom, as if He were a husband away at war.

"Do you know Jesus, Billy?" she'd asked when he first came. "Do you know Jesus?"

Billy nodded. He'd been to Sunday school a few times and heard the name. But his dad hadn't cared much for church and made jokes about it, so his mom hadn't taken him very often, and Billy soon found out that he didn't know Jesus near as well as Aunt Fay intended for him to. Soon he discovered he was full to popping with sin, like a pimple all pumped up with pus. And even Aunt Fay, holy as she was, was just a sin looking for a place to be committed. Evil was as much a part of being a human being as needing the bathroom. *"I am sinking deep in sin, far from the peaceful shore . . . ,"* the song went. And for eleven years this Billy, the one who knew all the hymns and sang them to the stars as he drove at ninety miles an hour down the nighttime highways, this Billy was raised by his aunt in the shadow of the cross, beneath the watchful eyes of six different pictures of Jesus, raised up to know a sin the way a hunting dog knows quail. *"Jesus loves the little children, all the children of the world . . . ,"* he learned to sing in his whiny, adolescent voice. And he believed.

The other Billy was a different animal entirely. As different as night is from day. His history started where the first's left off. At fifteen, Billy was shrunken and pruney, like a little old man in a child's clothes, slow to develop in every way. Some thought he was stupid, a moon-eyed boy who could rattle off the books of the Bible by heart but couldn't do long division or throw a baseball from home plate to first base, a kid who was afraid to smoke a cigarette behind the gym with the other boys and who ran from girls as if they were carriers of the plague, a boy who'd never drunk a beer. And then in one year this boy cracked open like an egg and a whole new person came out. Suddenly Billy Bumpus made the personal acquaintance of the sins Aunt Fay was talking about all the time. Not little-bitty sins like not brushing his teeth before going to bed and not keeping his room picked up but bigger stuff, stuff so big and powerful it nearly blew him apart: like girls who weren't miniatures of Aunt Fay and who knew how to do things that Billy didn't even have words for till they taught him, like drinks that he'd always been told would make him insane but that, when he tried them, only made him reckless and overflowing with a wild, animal energy. And stealing. And lying. And ideas that had nothing at all to do with the self-denial he'd learned at home. Suddenly the six different pictures of Jesus that hung around the house began to stare down at him like they'd never seen him before. This was the new Billy—sixteen years old and wild as a peach-orchard boar.

Fights followed this metamorphosis, with Aunt Fay quoting Bible verses at him as if they were magic spells that would put him back the way he'd been, and Billy throwing his own Bible verses right back in her teeth, like those soldiers in *Sergeant Rock* comics who tossed enemy grenades back into the German trenches before they could blow up. She told him he couldn't go out of the house except to school and church; he went where he wanted and quit going to church entirely. She forbade him to see his new friends; he saw who he pleased and came home drunk from their parties. She laid down deadlines and curfews for him; he stayed away all night and came home with suspicious stains on his clothes and the furious fathers of young girls in hot pursuit. And finally one Wednesday night while she was at midweek prayer meeting, praying for his soul no doubt, he left for good, just packed a duffel bag and disappeared. Bad, bad Billy Bumpus, down the road and gone. Where oh where did good little Billy go?

Once he was on his own, he learned to fend for himself pretty quick. The Lord helps those who help themselves. He could push a broom or handle a shovel or mix cement or stock shelves or pump gas or pick fruit or chop cotton or steal. And he could drive, although he had no license yet. He did all these things, this new Billy. He got by just fine. He learned how to fight and paid for the lessons with a few broken teeth and a couple of busted knuckles. Cheap at twice the price. But most valuable of all, he learned how to dance. Dancing was one of the last sins to fall because it involved potential public embarrassment. But Billy discovered that if he could dance he was welcome in any country-western honky-tonk in the world. Women would let him talk to them and touch them, and often enough let him go home with them. And all he had to do was dance like the Devil. So he learned the Texas two-step and the Cotton-Eyed Joe, the waltz, the western swing. . . . It was easier than fighting, and the payoff was a lot better too. Through dancing, the line of succession that had begun with April Metuchin on a stack of old *Life* magazines in the corner of her parents' garage lengthened to include all sorts of women, women who would take him in and feed him, bed him, look after him, tell him their life stories, and who sometimes told him to call them up when he came back through town.

Traveling was the other thing Billy did. Stealing cars led, through a complicated series of events, to driving delivery trucks, and that and hitchhiking led to a job driving the big rigs. And finally all that got Billy into the old Peterbilt with the serial numbers mysteriously filed off the engine, the one he was driving toward California now. Billy became a long-haul trucker and a short-haul lover. A dancing fool. Every married man's nightmare. The very person Aunt Fay had warned that other Billy about: a man highballing it full tilt down the wide highway to Hell.

Sometimes it worked out pretty good, though. He met some real nice ladies, and some of the ones who weren't so nice had friends who were, or daughters. But sometimes it didn't work so well. Sometimes there were screaming kids or husbands due back at 6 A.M. And he figured someday he'd get caught, either by a jealous husband coming home two hours early or by some sad, angry woman who'd wake up in the middle of the night and regret what she'd done and decide it was all his fault. Maybe it was like what Brother Ray Bob said—there would be a dangerous detour on the road of life. Maybe it wouldn't be a crash after all, as he'd always thought, but instead it would just be going to bed in a strange room some night and waking up looking down the barrel of a gun, the exit from this world reduced to a small, round hole. The old Billy Bumpus, the churchgoing one, thought about this now and then. Sometimes he envisioned himself at the gates of Heaven trying to finagle his way past Saint Peter the way he occasionally got past bouncers. Maybe he'd saved up enough goodness when he was little that there wouldn't be any trouble. Or maybe he'd just end up as another fish frying in the Lake of Fire.

He'd had a little insight into what that would be like once.

A couple of years ago, up in southern Idaho, he'd rounded a curve and seen an overturned semi down the hill. It was a big cab-over Freightliner that'd passed him twenty miles earlier. He slammed on his brakes, turned on his flashers, and jumped out and ran down toward the wreck. The truck was leaking diesel from the big tanks on either side of what had been the bottom a few minutes ago but was now, in this inverted position, the top. Billy smelled the fuel from forty yards away. He stopped and looked at the crushed cab and shattered windshield and wondered if the driver was still alive in there. He hoped the man was dead, but he couldn't tell. He might have been hanging there by his seat belt with his arms busted, unable to free himself. But even if Billy'd been sure of that, there was no way he was going any closer. The fuel was running down over the hot exhaust stacks and would go any second now. For a minute he ran back and forth, wishing somebody else would come and do something, but no one came. Then, first with a puff, then a huge flash and explosion, the fuel caught, and in an instant the truck turned into a sort of portable hell. He could feel the heat on his face, and the roar of the fire filled his ears. A solid cloud of black smoke rose up into the sky like a genie.

Billy watched the cab for a sign of movement but didn't see any. So after a minute he turned to go back to his own truck, anxious to put some miles between himself and the inferno, thinking he'd stop in the next town and tell somebody. But when he turned around, there was the driver lying behind him, under a little ledge where he'd apparently been thrown when the truck flipped. Billy must have stepped right past him coming down the hill.

The man was conscious and watching, but he couldn't say anything because his jaw was busted and blood was bubbling out his nose and mouth with every breath. Billy looked at him for a minute and knew the man had seen his cowardice, had followed his entire train of thought from the leaking fuel to the suddenness of death to Eternal Damnation. And the idea that the man could have seen all this was almost as frightening as the burning truck. But something in Billy was irritated by it too, and he didn't want to let himself be caught twice. So either the Good Billy wanting to do the right thing or the Bad Billy wanting to show this hapless dying bastard that he wasn't chicken made him go over to the man instead of leaving him to die on his own.

"You okay?" Billy said, realizing soon as he said it the utter stupidity of the question. The man was about to die. His lungs were punctured, his arms and legs were twisted around funny, and from the way he was lying, his back was broken too. He had an appointment with his Maker any minute. But from his position, balanced there between this world and the next, the man managed a slight smile at the dumb remark. He was probably an okay guy and Billy wished he could help him somehow.

"Is there anything I can do for you? I got some beer in the truck, if you're thirsty. Ain't got no water, though," Billy said.

The man's eyes said no thanks.

"I could go get help in Franklin. I think it's about forty miles. Maybe there'd be a doctor or something. With that fire burning, anybody else comes along here'll see you and stop. But I'm afraid to move you. You're too busted up."

The man's eyes stayed on Billy's face, understanding every word, knowing there was no time. His breath began to gurgle a little.

"You religious?" Billy asked at last. "I used to pray some. I could pray if you want."

The man's expression didn't change.

Billy closed his eyes and tilted his face up to the cloudless blue sky and prayed:

"Dear Jesus, please help this busted-up truck driver in his hour o' need. Ease his pain and calm down his fear and make him comfortable here on the ground. He's bound to have friends who care about him. Maybe a wife and kids too. So please, Lord, help him some if You can. Amen."

It wasn't much of a prayer really. Not like the beautiful ones he used to hear in church. And saying it was like talking in a foreign language he used to know. But it was okay. When Billy looked at the driver again, the man's eyes had lost their expression. His gurgling breath had stopped.

Billy got up and went back to his truck and drove on to Franklin and reported the wreck to the sheriff there. When they asked him to fill out some forms on what he'd seen, he said he needed to go to the bathroom and slipped out and drove away. It wouldn't have done any good anyway. The man was already dead.

This experience did not stop Billy from living how he lived and doing what he did; he kept dancing and chasing women as hard as ever. But it made him think. And thinking about that made as much sense as thinking about what he'd do if he won the lottery. More. 'Cause everybody died, but nobody Billy knew had ever won a thing.

Up ahead a truck appears, coming toward him through the dark. Its lights blink. Billy answers with a blink of his own. Then, with a closing rush, they disappear into each other's rearview mirrors. "Hello," the lights flashed. "Hello yourself," Billy flashed back. End of conversation.

… **3** …

Lucinda Sue Ghertz

Lucinda Ghertz had long, shapely legs, red hair that hung down past her shoulders, and the sort of figure that made men turn to get a second look. And she had eyes the color of spring grass. Unfortunately the left one did not move in its socket but pointed always at the same spot, like a headlight—just below level and slightly to the left. Among all her physical attributes, only that eye seemed to fall short of perfection. So by the time she was thirty-three, unmarried, unloved, and still hanging out at Merton's Bigger 'n Dallas, where the truck drivers, cowboys, dirt farmers, pool shooters, and other assorted disenfranchised folks drank themselves back to what they thought was humanity, she had decided that that unmoving eye must be the cause of all the problems in her life. Every time she would meet a new man she would try to put him directly in front of that eye so that he wouldn't notice it didn't move. She would lean her head back slightly and turn so that he was ten degrees to her left, exactly in the center of the eye's fixed vision, and she would try to keep him there as if she had him caught in a spotlight. If he stepped to his right, she stepped to her left. If he stepped the other way, so did she, aiming that eye at him as if she were sighting a fleeing jackrabbit down the barrel of a gun. While this was going on, she would try to distract him by keeping her best and biggest smile on her lips. But this expression—eyes fixed, smile painted on—only made her look like a badly designed doll. Locked in on her prey like a heat-seeking missile, she would shift and turn, shadowing his every move, smiling all the time, until finally the man would forget all about her lovely figure and her shiny red hair and he would begin to wonder whether maybe there was a windup key sticking out of her back or a cord connecting her to a power outlet in the wall. Anybody watching would see the two of them—Lucinda and whatever man she'd latched on to for the evening—moving slowly around like two people doing some strange dance, the man getting more and more nervous all the time and Lucinda's smile spreading and spreading until you thought her face would split. Unless the man had had an awful lot to drink, he wouldn't be able to stand this very long. Most of them finally bolted and ran—"Well, I gotta be going," and they were gone, sweating like they'd been under an interrogator's lamp—but some of them drank themselves into such a state that they wouldn't have cared if Lucinda was an investigator for the Internal Revenue Service; they just dimly saw her as a sort of generic woman, something to go home with.

So eventually Lucinda became convinced that the only men she could get were drunks, and she blamed it all on that eye. "Damn you!" she'd yell at the reflection of her eye in the mirror. And then tears would seep out of it, just like the other one, leaving little black trails of mascara down her cheeks like the smoke from a shot-down airplane. But every weekend she would go back over to Bigger 'n Dallas and do it all again, because she couldn't think of what else to do.

Once, a long time ago, she had moved to Denver for a year, but the winter was too cold and she didn't like the traffic and she couldn't figure out what shops to go to for anything and nobody knew her. She'd become a regular in the biggest country-western bar she'd ever seen, but the men there were the same as back in Tyrone. Maybe worse. So finally one day she got in her old Chevy Nova and pushed it back down I-25 toward home. "Too damn cold," she'd tell her friends when they asked her why she'd come back. "And you wouldn't believe the traffic." She wouldn't say anything about the way people had looked at her eye. She never said anything about that.

When she got back to Tyrone, arriving late one night, after the traffic signal had already changed from green-yellow-red to red-red-red one way and yellow-yellow-yellow the other (she approached from the yellow-yellow-yellow direction and considered it a bad omen), the town seemed to have shrunk while she was gone. It was as if it had been replaced by a miniature of itself, something built to two-thirds scale. The streets were narrower, the trees more scraggly, the streetlights fewer and dimmer than she'd remembered them. She drove straight to the home of her best friend, Judy, and switched off the engine and sat in her car, listening to the ticking of the cooling metal and the sighing of the late autumn wind. There was a light burning dimly in the window of Judy's trailer.

Lucinda hadn't thought to call ahead and say she was coming. Somehow she'd just assumed that everything had stayed the same in Tyrone after she'd left, and a part of her half expected to find Judy wearing the same gingham shirt and jeans she'd last seen her in. But now, as she sat there in the dark (she held her watch up in the light from the streetlight on the corner—it was nearly 2 A.M.) she realized she probably should have called. Well, what the hell, she figured. There was nothing she could do about it now. She didn't want to go to her sister's house. She and her sister Diane hadn't spoken since their mother had died, and two o'clock in the morning on a Thursday night was no time to try to patch up family problems. So Lucinda pushed the car door open and unfolded herself from the front seat into the cool night wind. When she closed the door, the sound set off the barking of a dog somewhere, and it made her remember that that was one of the constant background sounds of Tyrone: hunting dogs, lapdogs, guard dogs, farm dogs, dogs that barked at events that took place beyond the horizon, on other planets maybe, barking as if they were celebrating historic events, the way people honk their horns on New Year's Eve, barking back and forth to one another as if they were spreading news, bark, bark, bark, bark, bark. But this time the bark lasted only for a minute and then died away like a phone that stops ringing when nobody answers it. Lucinda arched her back and felt the vertebrae realigning themselves like boxcars in a long train that's starting to move. Then she stepped up the narrow cement walk that led to the door of the trailer.

Judy's father owned this lot. He had gotten it in some sort of trade years ago and had loaned it to Judy to live on. He wouldn't let her put a house on it, though, which was just as well because she couldn't have afforded one. She had picked up a secondhand 10x72 when everybody was trading up to double-wides, and she'd had it set up way at the back of the lot, against the alley. Because of this, the walk from the curb to the front door was twice as long as it should have been. Lucinda could hear her boot heels count off every step. Halfway to the trailer was a fiberglass birdbath, dry and with rings of sediment in it, standing like a broken promise to the birds. Lucinda remembered when Judy had bought it on sale at the Globe Discount Store in Lubbock. It was the same day Lucinda had bought a bed tray for eating breakfast in bed.

She pushed the lighted doorbell, two longs and a short, her ring since she was in high school. She could hear it buzz inside. After a moment there was the sound of feet and then a voice through the door.

"Who is it?"

"It's me. Lucinda. Open up."

And the door opened. There was Judy, barefoot, with her blouse buttoned crossways and her hair tossed. Behind her was a man sitting on the little couch. Lucinda heard the flick of a cigarette lighter as he lit up.

"Lucinda. Where did you come from? I thought you were in Denver."

"I was," Lucinda said, "but I'm not anymore. I'm back."

After a moment's hesitation, Judy opened the door the rest of the way and Lucinda climbed up the two steep wooden steps and came in.

"When'd you get to town?" Judy asked.

The man on the couch had his shirttail out and Lucinda noticed his pants were unzipped. After he'd taken a drag on his cigarette, he leaned back and zipped them up noisily.

"Just now. My stuff's in the car. I just drove in."

At the sound of the zipper, Judy remembered her manners and turned to the man on the couch. "Lucinda, this is Billy Bumpus. Billy, this is Lucinda Ghertz. You heard me talk about her."

Billy nodded amiably through his cigarette smoke.

"How long you going to be around? Where you staying?" Judy asked.

"I'm moving back. I was wondering if maybe I could stay here for a while."

Judy cast nervous glances back and forth between Lucinda and the smiling Billy Bumpus. "I . . . I guess you could stay on the couch. Me and Billy . . ."

"Naw, shit, any friend of yours can sleep with us," Billy Bumpus said, laughing. Lucinda looked at him again and noticed the way his eyes were glazed.

"Look," Lucinda said, "I can find someplace else. I didn't realize . . . I should have called and told you I was coming."

"No, where would you go at this time of night? You can stay on the couch. Billy's just been staying here for a couple of days till Smiley's gets a part for his truck. He'll probably be leaving soon. It's okay," Judy said. She and Lucinda looked at each other a little sadly, and then Judy said, "We'll talk some in the morning, okay? It's good to see you again." Turning to Billy, she said, "Come on. Let's go to bed. Lucinda'll be tired."

Billy stood himself up from the couch, rising slowly and unsteadily like a charmed cobra from an Indian's basket, looking at Lucinda all the time with a wet smile. "Sure you don't want to join us?"

"I'm sure," Lucinda said.

Then, just as he stepped past her in the cramped living room, he said, "You got somethin' wrong with your eye?"

Judy jerked his hand hard and they went together down the narrow passage that led to the bedroom in the other end of the trailer. "You know where everything is, Lucinda. I'll see you in the morning. Glad to see you," she said over her shoulder.

Lucinda brought her little blue backpack with her overnight things in it in from the car and put a blanket on the couch, and after brushing her teeth she took off her boots and blouse and jeans and went to bed. In the quiet dark she could hear Judy and Billy making love in the bedroom, but beyond that there was nothing. The trailer could have been a space capsule. In Denver, just before she'd left, she'd thought about being back, imagining the feeling of having her old friends close by and Tyrone spread out all around. In her mind it had somehow seemed like being wrapped in a thick quilt on a cold night. But now that she was back, there was nothing; just moaning and muttering from the bedroom, and a dark universe that came right down to the thin walls of a trailer that didn't belong to her. The blanket wasn't very thick and she was cold. She huddled against herself and went to sleep.

Sometime in the night Billy Bumpus climbed under the blanket next to her. He didn't say anything, and she didn't say anything. In the cold room his body was as warm as a heater. His hands were rough and his kisses tasted like flat beer, but she let him touch her and let him kiss her, and when he climbed on top of her she let him do that too because she was angry and disappointed and lonely and sad and wanted something specific to attach these feelings to and knew that letting this drunken redneck screw her would provide that focus. So she held on to him the way a drowning person holds on to a piece of wreckage, even if that piece of wreckage can't possibly hold her up, even if that piece of wreckage is waterlogged and sinking too. Just to hold something. And afterward, when he got up and walked back to the bedroom without saying a word, leaving her uncovered against the cold of the room and a wet spot on the couch cushion under her, Lucinda lay there thinking how it was not only the buildings in Tyrone that had shrunk while she was gone but the people too. If only Judy had been alone when she came, it would have all been different. But instead it was all the same.

The next day, Lucinda washed her hair and put on her best clothes and went to see Mr. Wild at the western-wear store. He said he'd put her on part-time. Then she found a place to stay, one of the rooms with a kitchenette at the back of the Drover House. And that night, which was a Friday night, she started going to Bigger 'n Dallas to drink and dance and meet men.

By the time a year had passed, she had a whole new set of friends. She and Judy had had a falling-out over who was using too much makeup, and now Lucinda only saw her old best friend across the width of the dance floor. Judy even drove over to Wilson to buy jeans rather than go in Wild Western, where Lucinda worked. The part for Billy Bumpus's truck had come the day after Lucinda had arrived, and he had taken off for California, where he'd been heading when he'd got stranded. Lucinda had never seen him again and didn't care to, even though she heard he came back through now and then. She saw enough like him every week. As time went on they seemed thicker and thicker, like flies swarming around something that's going bad.

Every Friday and Saturday when she'd leave the shop she'd go home and peel out of her work clothes (she was assistant manager of Wild's now—a career woman—and lived in a house she rented from her boss) and she'd soak in a tub of scented bubble bath and listen to whiny country-western music on the Lubbock radio station. Then she'd dry herself off and start getting ready for the night's dancing and drinking. She'd take about an hour picking out her clothes, because working in a western-wear store she had plenty to choose from. And then she'd spend another hour fixing her hair. And then she'd spend another hour putting on her makeup. She had decided that by using enough eyeliner and trying to keep herself in profile she could minimize the effect of her bad eye. And she also thought it gave her a haughty, go-to-hell look like some Hollywood type. She had arranged extra mirrors around her dresser among the pictures of Porter Waggoner and Conway Twitty and Hank Snow and Patsy Cline so that she could view herself in profile—right side only. She'd suck in her stomach and tilt her chin up slightly and look at that beautiful stuck-up bitch in the mirror and say, "What makes you so hot? Huh?" And then she'd put on a little more eyeliner, pretending not to see the creeping wrinkles that were eroding their way around the corners of her eyes and mouth like little gullies in the corner of a field.

All this careful preparation still left her ready for Bigger 'n Dallas about an hour and a half before anybody but the serious drunks would be there. So she would sit on her couch and watch TV.

Lucinda never ate before going to the bar. She said being

empty made her dance better, but it also made her stomach lie flatter under her jeans and it made the alcohol go to her head faster. The alcohol made her eye less important and the men less critical and the music better and the dancing freer and the laughter easier and the night shorter. The other thing it did that wasn't so good was if something *did* get to her—if some man said something about her eye or looked at it funny, or if she saw Judy dancing with somebody she wished she was dancing with—the alcohol made her get real mad real quick. But she couldn't understand how people who didn't drink could live. How could they face things?

On weekends Bigger 'n Dallas always had a live band. Sometimes it was the Rangers from Big Spring, and sometimes it was the Western-Airs from Amarillo and sometimes it was the Tumbleweeds from Lubbock, all of them good bands—voices like coyotes, and fiddles and guitars and wild, swooping pedal steels. The Western-Airs had a girl singer named Lily Gillette, who could get tears out of a dead man the way she sang "Restless Wind" and hearing it made Lucinda wish she could sing with a band. She didn't have a bad voice. Once the leader of a band from Oklahoma called Stampede had asked her to get up and sing a number with them, but she'd been too nervous. Later that night she'd lain in his arms and dreamed about singing with a band at the Grand Ole Opry. In her dream she wore a wide glittery skirt that stood out around her like an island that nobody was allowed to land on, and her voice went into the microphone and came out all the radios and TVs of everybody she'd ever known, everybody who'd ever looked funny at her. She was in profile and the spotlights sparkled like fire in her red hair. "Your cheeeaaatin' heeeaaaaarrrt will tell on yoooouuuuu . . . ," she sang, accompanied by a huge orchestra of fiddles and pedal steel guitars with their strings shining like railroad tracks in the moonlight, all played by men in tuxedos. Amid the wild applause that followed, she woke up to find the bandleader digging through her dresser drawer looking for her wallet. She'd taken out the pistol she kept under the edge of the bed and made him leave, made him put his clothes on outside in the front yard, and after he was gone she'd cried and wished she'd shot his worthless ass when she'd had the chance. But by the end of the week she couldn't even remember his name.

By the time she got to be thirty-three, Lucinda had her life down to a pattern so set that she could go from week to week without ever having to think about it. Mr. Wild thought she was "sane and sensible" except for her weekend exploits, which came to him in whispered communications from his wife, who hated Lucinda and who heard about these "shameless flings" of hers at the beauty parlor. But Mr. Wild knew he couldn't run the shop without a good assistant manager, or if he did, he'd have to work a whole lot harder and not spend so much time taking coffee breaks with his pals. So he told his wife (Lucinda had overheard him through his not-quite-closed office door) that what Lucinda did with her own time was her private business as long as it didn't cause trouble in the shop. And it didn't cause trouble in the shop at all. In fact, all the cowboys who hung out at Bigger 'n Dallas came in just to see Lucinda. She was notorious. But she wouldn't talk to them unless they were buying stuff, so all her conversations were carried on to the tune of the ringing cash register. Mr. Wild would have been crazy to get rid of her, and he knew it. So her position with him was secure. Everything in her life was secure: her house, her pickup (a pink International Harvester quarter-ton), her eight pairs of cowboy boots, her ten dancing skirts, her twenty pairs of blue jeans, her thirty-five western shirts, her six Resistol hats in different colors and shapes with feathers and rattlesnake bands, her daily and weekly and even monthly schedule (thanks to the Pill), everything, *everything*, was as secure and regular as life after death. So when, on Friday nights, she drove out to Bigger 'n Dallas, scrubbed and hungry and ready to dance, the only surprise ever waiting was who would disappoint her next. At thirty-three, she looked back on a life as featureless as a well-planned parking lot, the only slight bump in it was the year she'd spent in Denver, and she'd almost forgotten about that now. And when she looked forward at the future, there was nothing on the horizon at all. It reminded her of the stories she'd been told in Texas-history class in high school about the early Spanish explorers and how they'd had to mark their way across the plains around Tyrone by driving stakes in the ground and sighting from one to the other as if they were planning a housing development. Sometimes Lucinda felt as if she'd forgotten to drive the stakes into her life and now she had no markers, like she'd accidentally circled back on herself so that forevermore she'd be walking into Bigger 'n Dallas on a Saturday night, hungry, lonely, horny, and ready for something that would never ever happen. Secure, like gold bars locked in a secret place until they were forgotten. Regular, the way old people always wanted to be. Thirty-three years old and counting.

Then one Saturday night she went to Bigger 'n Dallas and there was a band from New Mexico called Sandstorm. They were two fiddles and two guitars and a pedal steel, just like everybody else, and all of them looked as if they'd been on the road since the time of Billy the Kid, except for one of the fiddle players, who looked just like Jesus Christ. He was young and wore sandals and ragged blue jeans and a leather shirt with a big green peace symbol on the back of it, and his hair hung down on his shoulders and he had a scraggly little beard. He didn't sing with the others, and when the leader of the band introduced the members, he said this boy's name was Freddy and he was just substituting for their regular fiddler, Bud, who was laid up in the hospital with a slight gunshot wound. Then they dedicated the next number to Bud's speedy recovery.

Sometime after midnight, when everybody in the place was pretty well lubricated and Lucinda had been dancing every dance with a tall cowboy from Garland who'd said out of the blue that he had to get the headlights on his truck aligned sometime soon, during a break between sets, somebody jumped up on the bandstand and started talking. At first it was just a joke, some guy who'd had a few too many and thought he'd solved the world's problems. The fellow talking was saying how he'd been in Vietnam where he'd fought for his country. This got a big cheer out of the crowd. Then he started talking about these so-called hippies—Commies who didn't think the United States of America ought to be trying to defend its little gook brothers but ought to just let the Reds get them. The next thing anybody knew he had the long-haired fiddle player dragged up to the microphone and was asking him, Didn't he think these so-called hippies were a load of crap? The fiddler's eyes were as big and white as a spooked horse's. He nodded at everything the cowboy said. Yes sir, yes sir, yes sir. But somehow the fellow talking made out that the fiddler was just putting him on, making fun of him, and would go out and tell all his hippie friends how he'd made a fool of a veteran of the Vietnam War if he got away. Now the fiddler was shaking his head the other way, no sir, no sir, no sir. Finally old man Merton had to come out from behind the bar with a sawed-off pool cue and stop the performance before it got out of hand. He got the speech-making fellow off the bandstand and got the band to playing again.

After a couple of numbers, the bandleader leaned over and said something to the hippie fiddler and Lucinda saw him nod back and slip off the stage. She figured he was smart for making his escape.

A little bit later she went to the ladies' room. After she was finished, she decided to step out the back door and have a smoke and cool off before going back for another dance. The temperature inside seemed to have climbed to about a hundred and fifty and she and everybody else were sweating like stokers. So she went out the fire exit and leaned against the cool cement-block wall and watched her cigarette smoke drift gray against the little white moon. She'd been standing there a minute when she heard a moan from the shadows at the corner of the building.

Over the years Lucinda had found all sorts of things out the back door of Bigger 'n Dallas—couples screwing, people fighting, drunks passed out, men pissing—and she'd got real good at minding her own business. But by the time she'd smoked her cigarette down to the filter, the source of these moans had begun to move, to sit up and say, "Oh, God. I'm dying. Help me." Lucinda took a last drag, crushed out the butt against the wall, and then, after hesitating with her hand on the door handle, she finally said, "What's the matter?"

"They beat me up. Busted my violin."

"You going to be okay?"

"I don't know. I think maybe my hand's broke." And then the voice was replaced by a series of sobs. In the dark she could hear him, although all she could see was a slight shaking of his body.

She stepped over to him and bent down. "You going to be okay?" she asked again, touching him just slightly on the back of his shirt, as if she were correcting his posture.

He shrugged and sniffed.

"You better get out of here before they come back," she said.

"I don't have anyplace to go," he said.

Lucinda had heard all the lines and had fallen for most of them at one time or another, but she had never heard this one delivered so convincingly. "I was just about to go home myself. I got a couch. I guess you could stay there tonight if you wanted," she said.

He nodded and wiped his nose and said, "Thanks."

She led him around the building to where her pickup was parked. By the light of the big neon sign, she could see that his nose was bleeding a little and he had dirt on his face. His beard wasn't thick, and in the hard glare she could see his features under it. He looked no more than twenty.

When they got to her house, she gave him a towel and he took a bath. It took him a long time. When he came out of the bathroom, he'd used a bunch of her bubble bath and about half a bottle of her favorite shampoo and cream rinse and his long dark hair looked like the coat of a Thoroughbred colt. He wasn't very tall and he was thin, as though he hadn't been eating well. She offered him a drink and he said he'd like some tea, that he didn't believe in alcohol. She snorted and made him some instant coffee. They sat at the breakfast table and talked while he sipped it noisily. Lucinda had a can of beer.

He told her his name was Freddy Steinberg and he was Jewish and was from Clovis. He'd only been with the band for three days, and this was his second job. He was planning to go up to Colorado and join a commune. Besides playing the violin (he never said *fiddle*), he did healing massage and vegetarian cooking and had once contacted the spirit of a dead person whose name was Leo. He thought he might have ESP too, but then he thought a lot of people had ESP and didn't know it because they let their negative vibes get in the way.

Lucinda told him how she'd been to Colorado once and hadn't liked it much. It was too cold. And she told him she worked in a western-wear shop and danced every weekend at the bar where he'd been beat up. He asked her about Colorado, and she started talking about the snow and ice, how she'd had to leave her car parked for a week once and hike through the snow to get anywhere, and how she'd sat in her basement apartment with the heater running, and how she'd been alone all the time. He said he liked snow and being inside when it was cold, but he could understand about being alone.

In an hour they were on the floor in the living room and Freddy was giving Lucinda a healing massage for her back, where it'd been hurting her low down. His hands kneaded her muscles, and warmth seemed to spread out from his fingers as he worked. He apologized for not doing a better job on account of his hurt hand, but she told him he was doing just fine.

When he was finished, he said he was tired and if she'd just show him where he could sleep he'd like to get some rest. He said she could leave the dishes from the coffee and everything and he'd take care of it in the morning. Lucinda smiled to herself and thought this must be the best line ever. Then she said she thought he might like to sleep with her. He looked at her very seriously, straight in the face for several seconds, and at first she thought he was looking at her eye, but then he said okay, and she knew he'd just been looking at her to see what she meant.

It had been a long time since she'd slept with someone who wasn't drunk, and it had been almost as long since she had slept with someone when *she* wasn't drunk. He was shy at first, and strangely enough so was she. Shy because she didn't want to reveal how experienced she was, shy because he seemed so serious about things. His skin was soft, and his hands explored like cats in a new house.

The next morning was Sunday. The recording of chiming bells that the First Baptist Church broadcast from speakers in the top of its little two-story fake belfry came into the bedroom in waves because of the wind. The wind was blowing toward town, so when it blew the chiming was blown back, but when the wind slackened to catch its breath Lucinda could hear the recorded bells again. She woke up with a feeling that she'd forgotten something, and she lay there trying to remember what it was until she heard a clatter in the kitchen. Then she remembered the musician who'd tried to steal her money and she rolled over and grabbed her pistol from under the edge of the bed and got up and pulled on her robe. When she went into the kitchen, she found Freddy, totally naked, standing at the stove over a skillet of pancakes.

"You're up," he said.

"Yeah. What are you doing?" she asked, hiding the pistol behind herself.

"Breakfast. I don't eat bacon and you only had white flour, but I thought maybe pancakes would be okay. I make pretty good pancakes. You like pancakes, don't you? I was going to bring it to you in bed."

Before the pancakes were done, she'd gone back to the bedroom and put the pistol away and then stopped in the bathroom and combed her hair and scrubbed all of last night's makeup off her face and replaced it with moisturizing lotion.

He was still naked when they ate. He didn't put on any clothes all day. Eventually he talked her into taking her clothes off—"Not to make love or anything, just to let your skin, like, breathe"—and they closed the front curtains and watched an old Charlie Chan movie on TV. "Like in a nudist camp," he said.

When the movie was over, Freddy started talking about how wise the Chinese were and how they recognized things and knew things that Western people (by which she thought he meant cowboys but finally realized he meant white people) had no idea of. According to him, the Chinese knew all about ESP and astral projection and reflexology and herbal medicine and all that kind of thing. Then he turned to her and said, straight out, "Can you see out of your left eye?"

Normally this would have made Lucinda want to kill him,

but he'd said it so conversationally—like he was just asking how she'd liked her pancakes—that she answered him: "Yeah. I can see fine. It just doesn't move, that's all. I had an accident when I was little, playing with my sister."

"So sometimes you can see two directions at once?"

"Yeah. If I'm not looking straight ahead with the other one."

"You're the only person I've ever met who can see what's in front of them at the same time they're looking around. You know, you're probably psychic. That eye is probably a symbol of psychic power."

"I don't think so," Lucinda said, looking away to hide her smile.

"How do you know?"

"Isn't being psychic the kind of thing people know about if they've got it? Like being tall or having big feet?"

"Not always. I was eighteen before I contacted Leo beyond the grave. I guess it could take even longer. Let's try something. I'll try to clear my mind of thoughts, and you try to tell me what I'm thinking."

"How can I tell what you're thinking if you clear your mind of thoughts?" Lucinda asked.

"I won't be able to get it completely clear, but if I try there'll be less clutter, so you'll be able to read it better."

So they tried it—Freddy with his eyes closed and his hands over his forehead, and Lucinda sitting next to him with her eyes open, perfectly still as if she were listening for the recorded church bells. She couldn't hear anything but the wind blowing against a loose windowpane.

Finally she said, "It's no good, Freddy. I'm not psychic. I'd have known it if I was."

"What do you think I was thinking? Tell me," he asked, opening his eyes and turning to face her.

"I don't know."

"Come on. Maybe you really know, but you don't think you do. Tell me what you think. Come on, try."

"Okay, okay." Lucinda closed her eyes for a moment, then said, "China."

"Right! Right!" Freddy said. "I knew it. You *are* psychic. You're just not developed. Your eye can see into people's minds and hearts. That's why it's like that. I knew it."

Lucinda laughed, watching him, naked, bouncing up and down on her couch, with his dark hair rippling over his shoulders as he nodded his head for emphasis.

"I'm serious about this, Lucinda. Really!" he said.

"I know you are." And she laughed even harder.

Freddy stayed on with Lucinda most of the week. When she'd go to work, he'd clean the house and cook strange vegetarian dinners with beans and rice and raw vegetables and loads of soy sauce. At night they'd sit naked in front of the TV and he'd tell her about how he thought the world didn't have to be as bad as it was if only people were more natural and loving and didn't drink so much and tried to get in touch with their real selves.

That Wednesday Lucinda left work a few minutes early saying she had an errand to run. She drove to the pawn shop and bought an old violin she'd seen hanging in the window, and that night she gave it to Freddy. They sat naked on the couch and he played sweet, sad music that brought tears to her eyes. She asked him to play "Put Your Sweet Lips a Little Closer to the Phone," and halfway through it she started singing, thin uncertain notes at first, but he smiled and nodded and her voice came stronger. *"You cain't saaaayyy the words I wanna hear, when sheeeeeeee is there with youuuu . . . ,"* she sang. Later they made slow love by the light of the *Johnny Carson* show.

The next morning Freddy asked Lucinda to come to the commune with him. She was just pulling on her boots to go to work when he said it. She looked up and he was standing in the hallway wearing his blue jeans, no shirt, barefoot.

"I can't, Freddy. This is where I live. I've got a job and a house and all," she said.

"But you've got ESP. You should develop it. Besides, you know more about Colorado than I do. We could drive up in your truck, and you could show me some of the places you remember."

"I hated it there, Freddy. That's why I came back here."

"That was a long time ago. It'd be different now. We'd be together. People ought to do something different once in a while. Besides, you don't even like it here. You told me so. Come on, Lucinda. Come with me."

Lucinda pulled on her other boot and stood up to look at her face in the mirror. Her right eye darted here and there—nose, eye, lip, chin, hair—but her left eye just stared straight at its own reflection, like always.

"Tell me what I'm thinking, Lucinda," Freddy said.

"I don't know what you're thinking, Freddy. I've got to go to work," she said, breaking away from her own one-eyed stare.

"Come on. Try. Just this last time. I'll be gone when you get home tonight."

He put his hands to the sides of his head and closed his eyes so that he looked like a drawing from a book on psychic energy. Lucinda looked at him, the bruised delicacy of his fingers, his flat, smooth chest, his long beautiful hair that had used up all her best shampoo.

"I'm going to miss you, Freddy," she said softly.

"That's right," he said, opening his eyes. "That's what I was thinking. How you're going to miss me. And how I'm going to miss you too. Come with me. With your eye, you could be a great psychic."

"And you could get a ride to Colorado," she said.

He nodded and smiled.

It was late afternoon as they approached the intersection where the farm-to-market road met the main highway going north. As they got to the intersection Lucinda pulled the overloaded pickup off the pavement and stopped on the dirt. Freddy had been riding with his head stuck out the window like a dog, his hair flying into shiny tangles. Now he turned and looked at her. She was just sitting there with her jaw clenched, staring straight out the windshield at the flat tan horizon, gripping the steering wheel hard as if she were going a hundred miles an hour. After a minute she reached down under the seat and began to grope around. When she straightened up, she had her pistol in her hand. She held it in her lap and looked at it for a few seconds. Then she opened the door and got out of the truck and took the jack handle out from behind the seat. Carrying the pistol and the handle, she climbed through the barbed-wire fence that bordered the road and walked twenty yards out into the empty flatness of the prairie. When she got there, she stopped and looked around, like she was alone, and then she stuck the jack handle into the ground and began pounding it down with the butt of the pistol until it stuck up about a foot and a half above the short grass. When she had done this, she came back to the truck and put the pistol back under the seat and started the motor and pulled back onto the road, turning north on the highway.

After they'd driven for a couple of miles Freddy said, "What'd you do back there?"

Lucinda didn't answer. She smiled a little, but she kept her eyes on the road ahead.

4

Ronney Lee Smith

"Like the Disneyland of Death."

The phrase had stuck in Ronney's mind like those tunes he sometimes heard on the radio and couldn't forget. A reporter from one of the TV networks had said it out like he was reading the headline from tomorrow's newspaper in the smoke of his cigarette. He'd come in that afternoon in a special helicopter with a cameraman and a sound man and a still photographer from UPI. He'd been wearing a tan safari jacket like Ronney remembered Jungle Jim wearing on Saturday-morning TV when he was a kid. The reporter and his friends milled around and shot a lot of pictures, and then he stood in front of the camera and talked seriously into its lens while Ronney and some of the other grunts watched. It was totally unreal, him talking to that lens and acting as if he didn't see them at all. Then later, after the camera was put away, when they were all sitting around smoking dope and telling lies, the reporter smoked some with them and told stories about those assholes back in Washington, how dumb they were and everything. He told the stories well enough that everybody laughed; even if he hadn't, nobody was going to tell him to shut up and buzz off, because everybody was hoping to get interviewed and get their picture on the evening news back home so their families and girlfriends could see them.

Anyway, somebody'd been talking about how unreal everything was, the jungle and the shooting and people getting blown to hell right in front of you. They'd said it was like Disneyland. The reporter had blown out a big cloud of smoke and said, "Like the Disneyland of Death," and everybody got real quiet for a minute because it sounded so nice the way he said it.

Ronney didn't remember much from the time he left the Real World until the time he got back, two years later, but he remembered that phrase. Oh, he remembered a few things okay—the funny smell of the jungle after it'd been napalmed, the way aerial flares came down trailing smoke, the way an M-16 felt on full automatic and how the ejected shells spun and caught the dappled light in the jungle, disappearing when they went through shadows, and then flashing through little beams of light like gold bees. He remembered a lot of boredom, and the feeling of having the shit scared out of him, and the way people sometimes screamed in much higher voices than you'd think. But he didn't have, like, war stories. Nothing like the ones he'd heard from the old guys back home who'd been in World War II. Maybe it was because he'd stayed drunk and stoned all the time. "Better Living Through Chemistry," they'd called it in 'Nam, quoting the advertising slogan of some big company. With all the beer and dope, the whole thing had been like one long dream. Unreal. And like in any dream, he'd done things he couldn't believe, and later, when he was back home, back in the Real World, he *didn't* believe. Not enough to tell anybody.

Mostly he'd just done like his friend Crawley had told him: "Keep a low profile. You keep your head down," Crawley said, "and the worst they can do is shoot your balls off. Hahahahaha." Crawley was from Elk City, Oklahoma, and was on his third tour in 'Nam. He loved it. He said he figured he might go on fighting after the war was over, just for fun, like Robin Hood.

Once Crawley and Ronney got put with a bunch of Marines temporarily. These Marines were serious fighting men. One or two of them had the ears of people they'd killed hanging on little strings around their necks. While they were there, Ronney got a package from his mother with some food in it, and one of the things she sent was a bag of Del Monte dried peaches. He got to looking at those peaches and decided they looked just like dried ears, so he took a bootlace and strung a bunch of them together and started wearing them around. Nobody thought much about it. They just figured he'd traded some beer for them as a souvenir. He was always stealing beer and trading it for something. He'd even traded for a Jeep once, but he ended up having to bury it out in the jungle because it turned out it was stolen, same as the beer had been.

Anyway, one night some of the Marines were playing cards in a tent and Ronney went in there out of his mind on half a case of Budweiser and four or five hours of dope smoking, and he started waving these dried ears around. Everybody told him to fuck off, that he was drunk. He said, Oh, yeah? and that the whole goddamn Marine Corps should fuck off. When they'd turned to look at him, in preparation for stomping his ass to mud, he smiled a crazy smile and started eating these ears, which weren't ears at all but just Del Monte dried peaches from his mama. After that, he could have walked naked through camp and nobody would have said a word to him except for "Hi, Ronney." They thought he was the baddest of the bad, the craziest of the crazy, a truly gifted grunt. Crawley laughed till tears ran down through his whiskers. A couple of weeks later he got blown up by a mine while he was out on recon. After that, Ronney just kept a low profile and hoped nobody'd shoot his balls off.

That was the only story Ronney had to tell when he got back to the Real World. Nobody was interested in it, though, because it wasn't brave or bloody or smart or sad. Probably because Ronney wasn't brave or bloody or smart, although a lot of the time after he came back he was sad. Most of the time, in fact, because when he'd gotten back to the Real World it didn't seem so real anymore. It was like coming out of a triple feature horror movie and finding yourself standing around in the dingy lobby of the local theater with it dark outside and the wind blowing and no way home but walking and even when you get there there won't be anything to eat and nothing to do and nobody to talk to. Unreal. Once when Ronney'd had R and R in Hawaii, he'd seen a deep-sea fish lying on the pier with its eyes popping out of its head and its body all swelled up like a balloon. Somebody had told him it was like that because it'd been brought up from under the ocean. Decompression, they'd said. Ronney thought about that fish sometimes, and once in a while he'd look at himself in the bathroom mirror and puff out his cheeks and bug out his eyes. It made him look the same way. And that was how he felt. Decompressed. Like he was about to explode.

Ronney got back to Texas in the middle of the summer. He'd flown to the Philippines and then to Hawaii and then to California and finally to Dallas. He didn't know what to expect coming back, but what happened was nothing. His corporal's uniform might as well have been a bus driver's suit. Nobody even looked at him. He'd written his old girlfriend, Geraldine Stewart, and told her he was coming, but he hadn't heard back from her. She'd never been much for writing letters. Neither had he. He'd told her if she wanted to come meet him in Dallas he'd have some money and they could stay in a hotel and see the sights. But it was a long way from Wilson to Dallas, at least nine hours if you took the bus, so when he didn't hear from her he just figured he'd see her back home.

The bus to Wilson left at one o'clock in the afternoon. It being summer, there were a lot of people riding—kids on vacation, old ladies traveling to see their grandchildren, some foreigners seeing the USA. The foreigners were a boy and a girl from France. They sat right across from Ronney and jabbered back and forth, talking through their noses that funny way they do. He listened to them while he watched the scenery unwind past the window.

Whenever the bus stopped to pick somebody up or drop somebody off, the heat from outside rushed in and overwhelmed the air-conditioning and made Ronney remember the jungle heat. But he remembered it as if it were something from his childhood. Here even the idea of a jungle seemed crazy. Any fool could see the whole world was nothing but plowed fields and blue sky held apart by never-ending rows of telephone poles. All you had to do was look.

That evening the bus climbed up onto the caprock, up onto the Llano Estacado. It was like going to another floor in a big building. First floor: different kinds of trees and lots of bushes, oceans way off somewhere. Second floor: dry creek beds, mesquite trees, plowed fields, the land going up and down slightly like the water in a bathtub when you move. Third floor: the caprock, total flatness like something that's been ironed and starched, a few Chinese elms huddled in little groups like refugees, fields the size of small countries. In Vietnam, Ronney'd sometimes dreamed about this country. In his dream he'd seen it as a patterned brown ocean with a few houses floating on it like cabin cruisers. And now he was on that ocean, sailing out to one of the remote islands in this big silver yacht of a bus. The land extended uninterrupted to the flat horizon all around like a floor without walls, like a pool table without cushions, like a slow brown ocean completely becalmed. He looked over at the French tourists. One of them was asleep. The other was frowning into a James Bond book.

In Big Spring he changed buses. He had a couple of hours to wait, so he went out and walked around town. The sun was going down; cicadas were buzzing like little power saws in every tree he passed. He found a drugstore and got a Bell Bar and walked around eating it, following the side streets back into the neighborhoods, looking at the flat houses with their air conditioners humming in the windows and their lawn sprinklers squirting invisible arcs in the long gray shadows.

The bus to Wilson was late, and its air-conditioning wasn't working. Everybody had their windows open, and the wind of seventy-miles-an-hour blew through the inside like the prop wash from a helicopter, picking up candy wrappers, covers of old magazines, and dust and whirling it all around in the bus. The wind and the dark made the trip seem exciting to Ronney, but most of the people went to sleep.

It was almost midnight when the bus got to Wilson. It stopped just long enough for him to get off, and then it was gone, leaving him standing beside the closed Texaco station.

"Mom?"

"Huh? Who's this? What time is it?"

"It's Ronney."

"Ronney? Where are you? You calling from over there? Oh, my God, what's happened, baby?"

"No, Mom. I'm at the phone booth beside the Piggly Wiggly. Can you come get me?"

"You're where?"

"Didn't you get the postcard I sent?"

"You sent a postcard?"
"Can you come get me? I'll wait at the Texaco station."

A year later Ronney was fixing trucks at Smiley's Truck Stop, between Wilson and Tyrone. It was like being a battlefield doctor. People didn't bring their trucks to Smiley's for an oil change and a tune-up. If that was all they needed, they'd wait till they got to a dealership in Lubbock or Midland. The trucks that came to Smiley's were those that couldn't make it any farther, that limped in or were towed in—ancient Freightliners with rust pits in their paint and blue smoke pouring out of their stacks, Jimmies with half a million miles on them and bald tires all around, Peterbilts that left footprints of oil as they crept into the garage, refugees from the age of dinosaurs driven by half-crazed gear-jammers with their eyes standing out on stalks from too many whites and too much truck-stop coffee, men who operated on twenty hours of sleep a week.

"When can you get 'er fixed?" they'd ask.

Ronney learned to look at the old trucks and try to gauge how much he could get by with.

"You got a lot of oil leaking out of that transmission there."

"I didn't bring 'er in for the transmission. It's the water pump, dammit. Just worry about that. I got a load to deliver. Ain't got time for nothing fancy."

The parts for these trucks were hard to get. Some of them were so old that the dealers didn't carry them anymore. But there was a wrecking yard in San Antonio called Truck Heaven that Ronney could get a lot of stuff from. They were used parts, and San Antonio was nearly four hundred miles away, but it was that or nothing, and they were cheap. He'd call up long-distance and talk to a woman there named Doreen and tell her what he needed. She always knew if they had it. She'd send somebody out to get it off one of the junked trucks in the yard and then send it to Ronney on the bus next day, C.O.D.

"Be a couple of days before I can get that part," Ronney'd tell the driver. "Got to come all the way from San Antone."

"Well, dammit all to Hell! What am I s'posed to do in the meantime?"

Ronney would shrug and climb out of sight under the truck, down into the oily darkness of his grease pit. The drivers would go off cussing and bitching about how there was no way for a man to make a living anymore.

Ronney worked with another mechanic named Bugs Leonard, an old guy with greasy yellow-white hair and two fingers missing from his left hand where he'd got them caught in the fan belt of an idling Kenworth one night twenty years earlier. Bugs started in the morning at eight and worked till five, and Ronney came at eleven and stayed till eight in the evening. Once in a while they traded shifts and did it the other way around. In the middle of the day, when they both were there, was when they pulled engines and did the heavy work. But most of the time they worked separately, talking back and forth from their grease pits like two women hanging out laundry in neighboring yards or two doctors working on adjacent operating tables.

Bugs had been in World War II and had fought with General Patton in France, which was where he'd started working on diesel engines. To hear him tell it, he'd killed upwards of a hundred German soldiers at one time or another. It was the highlight of his life, and he talked about it all the time. Occasionally he'd stop between his war stories and ask Ronney about Vietnam. Ronney'd just shrug and say, "Aw, you know how it is." One day Ronney told him the story of the dried peaches. Bugs said, "Dried peaches, huh? I saw a lamp shade made out o' human skin once. Had tattoos all over it. Real pretty." And he launched off into another story from the Big War, the Good War, the one Ronney had read about in comic books as a kid. To Ronney it sounded like a war held under ideal conditions, like a baseball game in a domed stadium, an old-timers' game played by guys like Bugs who all got a nice round of applause when it was over.

Ronney lived with his mother for a couple of months when he first got back, but the old house seemed awfully small. He didn't seem to be able to get away from her no matter which room he went to. So that fall, after he got the job at Smiley's, he rented a little house on the outskirts of Tyrone, thirty miles away. He shared the house with a dog named Mike that Mrs. Smiley had given him, a puppy from her mongrel bitch, Fluffy. The house came partly furnished with a raggedy armchair and a matching couch (one end of which had to be propped level with three *Popular Mechanics*), and a dinette table with a single chair. He intended to get rid of all that and get some decent furniture someday, but all he managed to do was get a used mattress that he slept on on the floor and a used TV that he bought from Bugs's nephew when he moved to Houston. The TV only got one channel, the other was just snow. It seemed as if the money he made disappeared before he could get around to buying anything real with it. Dog food, beer, hamburger meat, gas for the '65 Malibu he drove ... dollars just ran through his fingers.

When he'd come back to town, he'd found out why Geraldine hadn't come to meet him in Dallas. She was gone. Gone to California with a guy she'd met at a football game, left on the back of a big motorcycle. Ronney'd called her house and her mother had told him. She said she still had his last letter if he wanted it back. And she said the picture on the postcard he'd sent was real pretty and was it really that green over there and did he have a nice time? Most of his other friends were gone too. Mark Humber was still around, working in the Wilson Feed & Seed, which his dad owned. But he was an even bigger asshole than Ronney remembered from school. Monroe Snyder was farming, married now to Carrie Wharton, who he'd been going steady with when Ronney left. There were a few others, faces he'd see on the street and recognize, names he knew. He talked to them if he met them, but that was about it. Their lives had gone on without him, and the space he'd once occupied was taken up now by somebody or something else.

He got to know the man who ran the Gold Key liquor store, on the edge of Tyrone, where he bought his beer. His name was Leon. Some nights when Ronney got off work, he'd stop by there and talk to Leon for an hour or so. Leon was about ten years older than him and wasn't married either. But he had a girlfriend named Lucille who came around the store sometimes and couldn't have been any more than seventeen. She was something. Long hair bleached whitey-blonde hanging down on either side of her face. Lots of makeup. Seventeen years old and on her way to thirty with no stops in between. By the time she really was thirty, she'd be like one of those trucks Ronney worked on: compression shot, tires worn down to the cord, paint job freckled with rust, and oil dripping from every seal—a woman in need of a complete major overhaul. She was living her life in the fast lane, pouring herself into every minute that came by. Hot stuff. She would come into the shop swiveling her hips in her skintight jeans, her little tits pressing against the front of her tight T-shirt like two friendly animals poking points into the cloth with their noses. She had it all and intended to use it up fast.

Leon saw the way Ronney reacted the first time he saw Lucille, and he just laughed. Lucille smiled and went over and stuck her long pink tongue in old Leon's ear and he squeezed her ass. Ronney ended up with a lump in his pants that made both of them laugh at him. He just smiled sadly and took his beer on home.

One night when Ronney went by the Gold Key, Lucille

came and he got so frustrated watching her he thought he was going to have a stroke or something. All the way home he had visions of Leon and Lucille getting it on in the stockroom between customers. It seemed like every car he passed had two people in it and only he was alone. When he got home, he watched TV for a half hour and killed three bottles of beer one after the other before he decided that if he stayed there any longer he'd end up killing himself too, so he showered, scrubbed off every speck of grease, shaved, splashed on about a half-pint of the after-shave his mother had given him for Christmas, and put on a clean pair of jeans and an almost-new cowboy shirt. Then he got in his Malibu and cruised out to a big cowboy bar he'd heard about on the edge of town to see if he could find somebody to talk to. Especially some women.

The parking lot was packed with a weekend crowd. This is where it is, he thought. There have to be some single women here. He could hear the music leaking out into the night every time somebody opened the door to go in. It was as if all the good times in the whole county were in this one place; the neon sign in the parking lot announced it in flashing, ecstatic colors:

Merton's
BIGGER 'N DALLAS
drinkin' and dancin'

Ronney, propelled along by visions of what the night might hold, got out of his car and marched toward the door of the bar, walking the way he thought a war hero ought to, like John Wayne.

The atmosphere inside the bar was as thick as motor oil—cigarette smoke and beer fumes and body heat and noise and free-floating lust and undirected enthusiasm of all kinds. And tamping it all down was the syrupy whine of country-western music, the passion and disappointment of guitars and fiddles and lonesome tenor voices from a band of middle-aged entertainers in string ties and three-tone cowboy boots.

Ronney made his way to the bar and ordered a double Jack Daniel's on the rocks because it sounded so good to say it. Not being used to hard liquor—he never drank anything stronger than Colt 45—he swallowed this off and was ordering another before the band could get out of one tune and into the next, and with every swallow his image of himself seemed to get more substantial, tougher, and require more room at the bar. After a little bit, he was surveying the men and women around him like a rich cattle buyer at the stockyard thinking of picking up a few head for his herd.

"You know . . ." he said to the man next to him at the bar as he neared the bottom of his second drink, "this is sure nothin' like Hawaii."

The man turned and looked at him. "You talkin' to me?"

Ronney signaled the bartender for another double and turned, leaning back against the bar on his elbows, to face the milling dancing crowd.

"Yeah, when you're just out of the jungle and you see those hula girls and those beaches and those pineapple drinks with the little umbrellas in 'em . . . well, it seems pretty nice. But deep down inside what you really want is just some bar-b-q and a good old Texas cowgirl and a tall glass of Jack Daniel's," Ronney said, feeling more at home every minute.

The man next to him turned and looked where Ronney was looking, trying to see if maybe he'd missed something, like an island materializing beyond the far wall perhaps. But all he saw was an old cowboy putting the moves on a woman with a beehive hairdo.

"You fight in 'Nam?" Ronney asked suddenly, as if he'd been accused of something.

"Korea," the man said, going back to his beer. "That was mine."

"I was in 'Nam," Ronney said. "Just got back last year. Here we are, two men, fought for America. Killed people even. And none of these people even know it. When I came back here, there wasn't even anybody waitin' for me. Nothin'. You know? My girlfriend had gone off with some guy on a motorcycle. It was like comin' back to nothin'."

The man nodded. "That's a bitch all right."

"Damn straight it's a bitch!" Ronney said, surprising himself with his vehemence.

"It's them hippies," the man said. He said it without looking at Ronney, as if he were confiding it to his mug of beer.

"Yeah?"

"Yeah. Get all crazy on that shit they smoke. Lose respect for everything. Think life's just one big dope party."

Ronney thought about all the dope he'd smoked in Vietnam and wondered if the guy could somehow tell. But everybody had smoked it. Like a party only with explosives, he remembered thinking at some time or other. He tried to remember if anybody had had any fun at the party. But the only person he could recall enjoying it was Crawley, and he was dead. Ronney decided it had been a bad party. The man next to him went on talking.

". . . plot to sap America's willpower. Dope makes people nuts. Makes you sterile too. Everybody knows that. And the hippies get all the women. So there's no more kids being born. It's a fact. America'll just die out if it keeps on. We'll go extinct."

The man was about forty-five and looked like a former athlete going to fat. His face was the color of boiled ham up to the point where it was shaded by his hat brim. On his little finger he wore a ring with a horseshoe on it set in diamonds. His eyes were bulging slightly, and Ronney wondered if he was decompressed also.

"None of these folks even want to hear about it," the man

went on, turning to face Ronney and gesturing at the crowd with his empty hand. "Their country's bein' stol' right out from under 'em. We're bein' wiped out like the buffalo. Two years ago I had a wife and two little girls. Then she started gettin' all sorts of crazy ideas from the TV and those magazines. Started criticizin' everything. Wadn' nothin' bein' done right anymore, 'cordin' to her. There was no reas'nin' with her. It was like she'd lost her mind from all these things she was seein' on TV—snotty Jew reporters tryin' to make people look like fools, nigger lovers, eggheads, bureaucrats, college boys that figured they knew ever' answer to everything.... Decided she wanted to go to college. Shit, I never went to college. I went to Korea instead. And ran a farm, and grew things, and made things. And she had kids and fed a family and looked after the house. But it wad'n' enough anymore. They took her away from me just as sure as if they'd come out and picked her up in a truck and hauled her off like a hog to market. Her and my two little girls. Now she's up there at Texas Tech studyin' *modern art* and paintin' pictures nobody can understan'. Hangin' around with guys that got hair right down to their asses. Been gone nearly two years. Ruined now. And the girls too. They were good little girls, but now they'll just be two more little hippies with their hippie mama."

Although the man's voice was conversational, Ronney could see veins standing out on his temples, and his eyes looked as if he'd been staring into the sun all day. Ronney couldn't understand some of what he was saying—about why his wife had run off and all—but the look on his face was something Ronney knew; something he sometimes saw in his mirror when he shaved.

He looked over the crowd again. They looked to him now like some sort of endangered species; Bigger 'n Dallas was like a game preserve or a zoo. Or maybe they were more like soldiers surrounded and outnumbered, holed up here in this country-western bar like Bowie and Crockett trapped in the Alamo. And the news reporters and politicians and intellectuals were outside, picking them off one at a time—this man's wife, somebody else's girlfriend, a farmer's son sent off to college to study Ag who suddenly grows a beard and switches to sociology, an independent trucker stuck in the middle of nowhere because some guy he's never seen a thousand miles away decides to stop making parts for his obsolete rig. . . .

Another double Jack Daniel's had somehow appeared on the bar next to Ronney's hand. He picked it up and went to work on it. Partway through it he noticed his drinking buddy's eyes were fixed on the stage where a guitar player was introducing the members of the band. Ronney looked and saw, right up there, right in the middle of those musicians, like a coyote hiding out in a pack of sheep, one of the very hippies they'd been talking about, a guy with hair all the way down to his shoulders and a scraggly beard, like Ho Chi Minh, raggedy jeans, sandals. . . . And when he turned around, there was a peace symbol, like the mark of the beast, on the back of his shirt.

"Look a' that," the Korea vet said slowly.

Ronney nodded.

"Christ Almighty! And he can just come in here like he owns the place."

The band started playing again and the crowd was dancing. The hippie fiddler sawed away and tossed his long hair like the Devil himself, and suddenly Ronney had a vision of him putting a spell on the whole dancing crowd with his playing, leading them out the door and up the road and away. The more he drank and the wilder the music got and the more people danced, the more Ronney became convinced that he and the big cowboy next to him were the only ones who understood the true peril of the situation, the only ones who could save this crowd of people from being taken over by the invisible enemy and turned into God knows what all.

When the tune was over, the band took a break, and Ronney stumbled his way through the crowd toward the stage. He climbed up on it and lurched unsteadily toward the microphone.

"I got somethin' to say. Somethin' important."

His voice sounded enormous coming back through the monitor speakers on the little stage. It echoed in his ears. Between himself and the lighted bar area at the back, where the big cowboy stood, there was a dark sea of faces, eyes reflecting the stage lights in little sparkles like the port lights in Saigon Harbor. He held on to the cool chrome of the microphone stand for dear life, the same way he'd once held on to his rifle.

"I just got back from 'Nam," he said, pushing the words out, hearing the strange sound of his voice dissipating slowly in the air like thin smoke.

A ragged cheer rose from the crowd, encouraging him to go on.

"There's a . . . there's a war goin' on over there. . . . People gettin' shot up. And since I come back . . . been a year now . . . I been feelin' . . . sometimes I been feelin' like the war's already been lost. . . ."

Silence. Only his own breathing and a drop of sweat making its way down the side of his face.

"I work all day tryin' to . . . to fix old trucks. And I cain't get parts for 'em. The people that are supposed to have the parts don't make 'em anymore. . . . All the things we used to believe in are bein' taken away. . . . Not just the trucks. All kinds o' things. When I went in the army, everybody thought it was a good idea. . . . Go fight the Communists. But when I came back . . . everything's different. Everybody's changed.

Some people don't understand what I was doin' over there. . . . Sometimes I'm not . . . sure . . ."

His train of thought was slipping away. His vision of how the newsmen and business executives and college professors had the bar surrounded seemed crazy now as he looked at the crowd. People were starting to talk to one another and laugh. The idea that he was making a fool of himself suddenly made him furious, like he'd been tricked again. Why couldn't he get his hands on anything?! Why was *everything* so damned slippery?!

He looked around and saw the hippie fiddle player standing in the shadows at the back of the stage and seized on him the way a trial lawyer would seize on a piece of incontrovertible evidence, yanking the fiddler forward by the arm.

"Here," Ronney said, all but lifting the musician off his feet to show him to the crowd. "Here's one. Look a' this."

Then, turning to the fiddle player, he said, "Tell 'em what's going on."

The fiddle player was trying to twist free, but Ronney held him with a grip like lock-jaw pliers. "You think we ought to be over there fightin' for America?" he yelled at the musician.

The fiddler nodded emphatically, rattling his head up and down.

"Fight the Commies? Give 'em hell? Kill 'em all?"

Maddeningly the musician kept nodding, agreeing with everything he said.

"No you don't!" Ronney said. "You're tryin' to make fun of me. You think you're smarter'n I am. You think this is all just some big joke and you're gonna have a laugh about it later."

Now the kid was shaking his head just as hard as he'd been nodding it, still refusing to show his true colors, refusing to be what Ronney knew he was.

Then an old man the size of a grizzly bear materialized out

of nowhere and took the microphone out of Ronney's hands. "You better go have another drink, son," he said. "Cool down some." He was holding a sawed-off pool cue in one hand, and he peeled Ronney's fingers off the hippie's shirt as easily as if they'd been a child's. "Now you let him go. I'm not gonna have any rough stuff in my place," the old man said. "I don't want to have to . . . ," and the hippie was free and back in the shadows again.

Ronney looked at the old man's face and knew he could talk all night and never make anybody understand what he was trying to say. Maybe *he* didn't even understand. Maybe he'd gone crazy at last. The old man pushed him gently but firmly toward the steps and down from the little stage, saying something over his shoulder to the musicians, who had suddenly reappeared.

Slowly Ronney made his way back through the crowd. He could feel everybody staring at him as if he were naked. " 'Scuse me. 'Scuse me," he said, going through them as the music started and they began to move. *"We don't smoke marywanna in Muskogee. And we don't take our trips on LSD,"* the band sang.

The veteran of Korea was still at the bar. He didn't say anything when Ronney stepped up next to him and signaled for another drink. Ronney wanted the man to speak, to tell him he hadn't really made a fool of himself up there. But the man just sipped his beer, looking down into his glass as if that were where his wife and daughters had gone. After a minute Ronney turned to watch the band. The pedal steel player was taking a solo and the guitar player was saying something to the hippie fiddler. The hippie nodded and started putting his fiddle away.

"He's leavin'," Ronney said.

"Huh?" the man next to him said.

"He's fixin' to take off," Ronney said, and nodded in the direction of the stage.

The Korea vet watched for a few seconds, then said, "I think we oughta teach that boy a lesson. That little queer made a fool outa you, soldier," the man said, looking at Ronney with eyes like pointing fingers.

Outside it was dark and cool. After the noise of the bar, Ronney felt as if he'd gone deaf when they stepped out. The breeze on his sweaty back cleared his head a little, and when they'd stood outside for a few minutes he started to sober up. The two of them were leaning against a beat-up old Cadillac parked near the side of the building where they could see anybody who came out.

"He'll probably try to sneak out that way," the cowboy said, nodding toward the back door.

They waited. Ronney wondered what was taking the hippie so long and was just about to ask if the big guy thought he was hanging around inside or they'd somehow missed him when he heard the back door open and a long-haired figure appeared at the corner of the building and stopped, a thin silhouette in the dark, violin case tucked under one arm. The silhouette turned to look up at the moon, then started toward where they stood in the shadow.

"Hey, you," the cowboy said. The words sounded like a dog's bark. The hippie froze. Ronney followed the big man toward him.

"You think you can make a fool of a man who fought for his country and get away with it, you little queer?" the cowboy said. "You think you can come around here with your fuckin' peace symbol and your fuckin' long hair and your fuckin' dope and your fuckin' Communism and make fun of us? You got another think comin', boy. And I'm gonna give you a nice long hospital stay to consider it."

As soon as the cowboy was in range, he reached out and punched the hippie in the stomach, knocking him back into the wall. The violin case fell to the ground. The cowboy looked at it for an instant, then raised his boot and crushed it. There was the sound of splintering wood and twanging strings as the fiddle disintegrated. The hippie, who had slid down to the ground now, reached out his hand toward his smashed instrument, but the cowboy kicked the hand away with a smack.

There wasn't much light behind the building, but Ronney could just make out the hippie's expression. He looked young and scared, not like inside. . . . In that instant between when the kid looked up and when the cowboy slugged him in the face, the whole scene seemed to Ronney like a dream he'd had before—the fiddler's dark hair and terrified eyes—something that went with being drunk and confused and scared. Then the boy was on his back, with his hands over his face, moaning. The cowboy was standing over him, breathing hard, drawing back his foot.

"Stop it!" Ronney said, as if it were him and not the hippie who was about to be booted in the ribs. He grabbed the big man's shoulders and pulled at him. "That's enough. It's enough."

The man turned around. Ronney could see and feel the pent-up energy in him. The throbbing line of a dilated vein ran from the black shadow of his hat down the side of his neck.

"He's just some stupid fiddler," Ronney said in a voice that would not stop shaking. "It's not him that's responsible for everything. It's not him took your wife."

"Well, who the hell was it, then?" the man shouted. The words hit Ronney's face in a hot vaporous blast.

"I don' know. Somebody else. Those guys on TV. . . ."

Ronney wanted to take the man by the shoulders and turn him away, but he was afraid to touch him again, afraid the vein in his neck might go off like the mine that killed

Crawley. He stepped between the cowboy and the kid and held his arms out like an usher. The cowboy looked at him for a moment, staring hard at him, then turned and walked unsteadily away. Ronney followed.

They crossed the wide dirt parking lot to an old Chevy half-ton stake-side in the corner. Ronney stopped beside the front fender. The cowboy went to the door, yanked it open, got in, and slammed it. The motor spun, caught uncertainly, then the headlights came on. For several seconds there was only the faint squeal of a loose fan belt, the ticking of a valve out of adjustment. Then the window rolled down. The man's voice came from behind the glare of the lights.

"I got a 30-30 in here. I could go back and blow that hippie's head off if I wanted to. . . . I could blow yours off too. Right where you're standing. Nothing to stop me."

Ronney stared into the darkness beyond the glare, wondering if the cowboy was reaching back now, taking the rifle from its rack, taking aim. . . . Then the truck jerked forward, kicking up dust as it went by. It passed so close that the side mirror almost hit him. At the edge of the parking lot the truck swung wildly onto the road that led away from town. Ronney watched its taillights shrink till they were just two red sparks in the dark.

After that, there was only the sound of a dog barking in the distance and the music coming softly through the walls of the bar behind him. He closed his eyes and listened and smelled the air in long, deep breaths. Then he opened his eyes again and scanned the horizon, ending with the neon sign. *"drinkin' and dancin'"* it said. *drinkin' and dancin' . . . drinkin' and dancin' . . . drinkin' and dancin'*. Blinking on and off. Better go see if that kid's okay, he thought, and started back across the parking lot.

Before he'd gone halfway, the kid came into sight, accompanied by a pretty redheaded woman Ronney'd noticed earlier dancing with some cowboy in the bar. He stopped and watched as she led the kid to a big pink pickup and helped him in. They drove away together. Ronney watched until they were out of sight.

None of it made any sense—him giving a speech, seeing that hippie as the Devil, the cowboy from Korea going crazy. And now the hippie leaving with a pretty woman, while he, who had saved the hippie's life, would go home alone to his ratty furniture and his cold mattress on the floor and his mongrel dog, who'd probably run off again like he always did. Ronney shook his head, shoved his hands down into the pockets of his jeans, and turned and walked to where his car was parked.

He drove home with the radio off and the windows down, smelling and tasting and listening to the night, feeling like he'd done something or seen something important but not able to figure out what it was.

5

Lucille Marie Wintergarten

Lucille Wintergarten looked at her reflection in the mirror. Her hair hung down past her shoulders, shining like metal wire. Maybe blonde wasn't her color. Maybe she should dye it midnight-black. Or fire-red, like it had been before. She wondered idly why there weren't other possibilities; blue maybe, or pink, or green. Why be stuck with just four colors of hair, why not lots of colors, like a butterfly? Lucille's natural hair color was mousy brown. Natural because that was the color it grew out of her head. But she considered that a sort of accident, like bad eyesight, and she didn't see any reason why she shouldn't have something that suited her personality. So now it was ash-blonde, because for the past few months she'd thought of herself as having a sort of ash-blonde personality—cool, sexy, mature, slightly tragic; the color of the moon, the color of morning frost. Ever since Julio had gone, she had felt her personal tragedy like a low-grade fever. She thought about dyeing her hair black now because that was the color his had been. She could make her hair into a sort of memorial: the Julio Romero Memorial Hair. Maybe not. Maybe ash-blonde was better. It went with her green eyes better anyway. And it made her tan look darker too.

She turned away from the mirror and picked a T-shirt out of

the pile on the floor. It was a child's T-shirt and fit like skin when she pulled it on. She'd wear a button-up dress shirt of her father's over it, and then in Texas-history class she'd unbutton the dress shirt like it was too hot for her and give old Mr. McDuffy a peek at her tits under that tight T-shirt. Make his eyes jump out behind his glasses like a pair of crash-test dummies. It was a game she played. He'd moved her to the front row of the class to keep her from talking to the kids around her, and she'd retaliated by seeing if she could give him a hard-on. She hadn't succeeded yet, but she'd made him blush twice already, and she'd made him lose his train of thought six times. Maybe that was all he could do, him being so old and all. Lucille thought about this while she pulled on her jeans and tennis shoes and her daddy's shirt, wondering exactly when guys lost it.

When she went into the kitchen, her father had already gone to work and her mother was talking on the telephone, like always. Lucille made herself a cup of instant coffee, dosed it with several spoons of sugar, and walked out of the house, drinking it as she went. Her mother was waving furiously at her, trying to get her attention and object to the way she was dressed and to the fact that she hadn't eaten breakfast, but as long as her mother was on the telephone—which was forever—she wouldn't stop and actually say anything to Lucille, and until she did Lucille would just keep on walking right past her like she wasn't there.

The morning was beautiful; dry, blue, not hot yet. Lucille inhaled deeply, feeling the clean air rush into her lungs. Then she dug her pack of Kools out of her big purse and stuck one between her lips and lighted it with an expert flick of the old Zippo she'd swiped from her mother's dresser drawer. She blew the smoke out through her mouth and nose all at once, like a dragon. The yellow Ford her grandmother had left her was parked against the curb, waiting to take her to school or anywhere else she wanted to go. Better go to school today, she thought, after briefly considering what would happen if she were to head for California instead. She got in and set the half-empty coffee cup on the dash, and as she drove she sang along with the Grateful Dead on the tape deck.

Julio had never liked the Grateful Dead. It was his one flaw. Other than that, he'd been perfect in every way—tall, quiet, dark, very handsome. And the fact that he was a Mexican and worked at her daddy's cotton gin jockeying the trailers around hadn't bothered Lucille at all. She wasn't prejudiced. In fact, if he hadn't worked there, she probably never would have met him. She met him one day when she'd gone to ask her daddy for some money to buy new clothes. She'd just gotten the Ford then—Grandmother Wintergarten had only been dead a month—and it had run out of gas right after she'd left the gin with a hundred bucks of her daddy's money in her pocket. So she called from a phone booth and her father told Ruben to send somebody to pick her up, and Julio was the one he sent, and that was how they met.

Julio was twenty and had just come to town to work with his Uncle Ruben, who'd been the press man at the gin for years and years. Julio was *so* handsome and had *such* sad black eyes and didn't know anybody in Tyrone except his old uncle. Lucille was sixteen and the boss's daughter. That day she'd seen herself as a sort of damsel in distress and Julio as her hero. He'd seen her as trouble and tried to keep his distance. But Lucille was not a girl to be put off. Not by him or anybody else. When she wanted something, she wanted it *right now*. Her mother said it was because she'd been fed on demand when she was a baby. Her father said it was because her mother and grandmother had spoiled her rotten on account of her being the only child in the family. Her schoolteachers said it was because she was immature. Lucille thought they were all full of shit. She was impatient because she expected to die a tragic death at an early age. The only person who'd ever understood her was Grandmother Wintergarten. She'd known that there was something special about Lucille, even if she hadn't known about the tragic death Lucille envisioned for herself. That's why the old woman had left her a yellow Ford coupe with only 22,000 miles on it when she died, so Lucille wouldn't have to wait so much. So she could get on with things. And Lucille did.

After she met Julio she started coming around the gin more often, sometimes on the pretext of seeing how her daddy was doing—a thing she'd never done before—and sometimes hovering around outside in the afternoons watching to see Julio's slightly stooped form come through the gate.

"Hey. You want a ride home or something?" she yelled out at him one day.

He looked around to see who she was talking to.

"You, Julio. I'm talking to you. You want a ride?"

"No. It's okay. I don't go far," he said in that soft, polite way of talking he had. Lucille just loved his accent.

"You want to go for a ride around then? Maybe get a Coke? We could drive over to the Whataburger in Neptune. I'm bored," she said.

Julio looked around again, then nodded uncertainly and came over and got in the car real fast, like he was expecting someone to try and stop him. Lucille could smell the sweat from his day's work when he got in. And she could see the nervous way he looked around—first at her, quickly taking in the tight clothes, the long hair (red at the time), and then looking away, as if the sight of her scorched his eyes. That first day they drove over to Neptune and she had a strawberry malt and some 'Tater Tots and he had a root beer. She asked him where he was from (Ozona was the last place he'd been) and where he lived (a converted garage behind his uncle's house), and she felt the eyes of the other people in the drive-in on her like spotlights. A white girl and a Mexican! Just imagine! Disapproval all around. Lucille knew that day that she was destined to fall deeply in love with Julio Romero, and there was not a damn thing anybody could do to stop her.

When she took him home, she insisted on coming in and seeing where he lived, because it was such a cute little place from the outside. He stood there in the middle of the single room with his hands in his pockets and his hair hanging over one eye, looking like a big kid. Lucille walked around looking at things, touching them—the little white wooden table where he ate and the stack of Mexican comics beside it, the upholstered chair with its stuffing coming out a little rip in one arm, the big mattress lying on the floor. The place was just perfect. He didn't have a TV, though, and she told him she could get him one. Her family had an extra just sitting out in the garage, gathering dust. He said no, that was okay, but she knew by the way he said it that she'd have to go get that TV and bring it back to him sometime, just to see him watch it with his big sad eyes. She could set it up across from the mattress and they could sit side by side and watch it together and she could explain any of the words he didn't understand. He thanked her for the ride and the root beer, and she made a point of touching his chest when she said good-bye. There were sparks between them, like touching an electric fence after a rainstorm, and she could feel his eyes on her back as she walked out to her car and drove off.

The next night, while her mother was on the telephone and her dad was watching TV, she went out to the garage and uncovered the old RCA that used to be in the den before they'd remodeled and put it in the car and drove over to Julio's house. He was so surprised to see her that he just stood there in the door. She finally had to tell him to move or she'd drop the TV and it wouldn't be any good to anybody. The night was hot, the beginning of September, and he was wearing a pair of old blue jeans and a pair of scuffed-up pointy-toed shoes and no shirt. His chest was like smooth mahogany, like a piece of old furniture, with no hair on it at all. After a minute he understood and got out of the way so she could come in.

He was going to put on a shirt, but she told him not to bother, she wasn't shocked or anything, and besides, it was real hot. It was so hot she wondered if he had any beer in the house, because she was just sweating up a storm from carrying that big old TV around. He jumped back and forth, not sure whether to help her with the TV first or get her a beer first. Finally she put the TV in the chair facing the bed and he got her a beer. The beer tasted great. Lucille wasn't supposed to have it, at least not legally yet. And now here she was, in a little house with a handsome half-dressed Mexican man who worked for her daddy, drinking cold beer and delivering a TV set her parents didn't know she'd taken. The evening heat came through the screen door, the soft dark hung beyond the open windows, cicadas buzzed like an orchestra of static from the pecan trees in the yard. It was delicious, intoxicating. She never wanted to be sober again.

"So, how you been, Julio?" she asked. "You look like you been workin' pretty hard."

He nodded.

"You want to, like, watch some TV or somethin'? It's a pretty good set, even though it's kinda' old. Used to be in our den before we remodeled and got a Sony."

She plugged it in and switched it on. After a moment, the screen brightened, rolled once, and then stabilized, slightly snowy. She adjusted the rabbit ears, improving the picture some.

"You got an outside antenna? It'd do better with that. It's a little funny with just the rabbit ears."

Julio said nothing but kept watching her. She pushed her hair back with one hand and turned her profile to him, knowing that was her best angle. She could feel his eyes on her, like a hand, like that time on the bus trip to see the school football game in Wilson last year when Jimmy Peters, thinking she was asleep, had put his hand on her knee and then slid it slowly up under her skirt till it was way up on her thigh—a touch that wasn't supposed to be a touch at all but was more than a touch because of that. Ever since that night two years ago when Lucille had looked at herself naked in the mirror and realized that the reflection there didn't match the way she thought she looked, there had been these moments. Although she never thought of it in so many words, she loved her new body, every new curve and swelling. It was as if somebody had suddenly replaced a dull, flat landscape with rolling hills, fertile and with lots of secret places to be explored. In some ways her body was like the yellow Ford, something she'd suddenly found herself in possession of and could use and enjoy whenever she wanted. But instead of gasoline, it was powered by the kind of looks she was getting now from Julio Romero, the kind of looks a hungry man gives a menu.

Lucille switched channels on the TV, noticing the way the light played on the backs of her fingers, on the skin of her thighs at the ragged edge of her cutoffs.

"Oh, here's a movie. You like movies, Julio?"

Now she looked at him, sipping her beer at the same time so that her gaze wouldn't seem so direct, wouldn't scare him off. His skin looked so dark and soft.

"You want to watch this movie? You mind if I watch it with you?"

The thing with Julio lasted nearly a month. She made up various stories about where she was going when she left home in the evenings. Sometimes she didn't come back till midnight. Most of her stories didn't hold up, and she had to make up new stories that were never even as good as the first ones. A couple of times she saw Ruben watching through his front window as she drove up. Julio was scared sometimes, but it only made him more passionate.

Then one evening at supper her father said casually, "Well, we had a little official visit at the gin today."

He was always saying things like that, trying to make what he did sound like it was a big deal.

"The immigration boys came around looking for wetbacks. Found one too. That nephew of old Ruben's."

Lucille's fork stopped with a load of steak halfway between her plate and her mouth.

"Yep," her father went on, clearly enjoying this, "hauled him off and shipped him away. Back where he came from. Probably halfway to Monterrey by now, courtesy of the U.S. government."

Lucille made herself put the bite of meat in her mouth. It tasted rubbery and vaguely dirty. For a minute she didn't think she'd ever get it swallowed, but she knew her father was looking at her, watching for her reaction, and she refused to give him one. She slowly finished her meal in silence, chewing each bite as if it were a piece of his hand she'd bitten off.

Later, when she was in her room, she stretched across the bed and stared at the ceiling, thinking, imagining her father meeting with various kinds of violent accidents but knowing that none of them would ever happen because he never did anything dangerous.

When she finally sat up, she had decided she wouldn't let him get the best of her, no matter what. The next day her hair went from red to ash-blonde. And she took some scissors and trimmed her cutoffs even shorter than they already were. And soon as she could she bought even tighter T-shirts from the children's department at the JCPenney's up in Lubbock. And she began the search for a new boyfriend—no, not a boyfriend, a new lover, someone her parents would *really* hate. Someone who would make them look back with nostalgic longing to the days when she'd spent her time with Julio Romero. She hoped Julio would write so she could write back and tell him how much she missed him and how brave she was being about it and how awful her father was, but he never did.

By a month later, when she turned seventeen, the real Julio seemed to have evaporated away, leaving behind only a sort of thin memory of gentleness and sexiness, like the irregular white halo left when a puddle of water evaporates. Oh, Julio, I miss you so much, she would say to the reflection in the mirror when she was feeling sad and lonely. Oh, Julio . . . Over and over, like she was talking to him instead of to herself.

In Texas-history class Mr. McDuffy said, "So the Spanish explorers were looking for the cities of gold, and they found themselves up on the plains, faced with what looked like an endless sea of grass. Can anybody tell me how they marked their way across it?" He paused expectantly, blinking behind his glasses. Lucille hated these little rhetorical questions of his. She'd been imagining the Spanish explorers driving up Highway 87 in their old Chevies on the way to the seven cities of gold. In her daydream Coronado was stripped to the waist and had the soft, dark eyes of Julio Romero. But now the image was gone. She looked at old McDuffy holding his little clawlike hands together in front of him like a hamster and smiling that stupid teacher's smile—"Who's going to be the good little boy or girl today?" That kind of smile. His glasses were so thick they made his eyes look like they were located in the back of his skull and looking out through tunnels in his head. Maybe that was why he was so dopey, like seeing fuzzy made everything else fuzzy too.

Lucille was idly following this line of speculation when Mr. McDuffy turned his little tunnel eyes on her and said, "Lucille, can you tell us how they marked their way across the plains?" He looked at her as if he expected her to break into song.

She slowly sat up and stretched, as if she'd been dozing. What was the answer to his stupid question? She knew she'd heard him say. He was always talking about the Spaniards, like it was a real *thing* with him.

"They watched the sun," she said. It sounded reasonable to her. "They navigated by the sun," she elaborated proudly.

"Ah, I can see some of us haven't done our reading assignment," Mr. McDuffy said in a singsongy voice, as if comforting a three-year-old. "No, they drove a line of stakes in the ground to mark their trail so they wouldn't get lost. They had to do this because there weren't any landmarks. The Great Plains were so flat and treeless they had to drive stakes in the ground to show the way back. That's why this area is called the Llano Estacado—which, as we all know by now, means 'Staked Plain' in Spanish."

Where did they get the stakes if there weren't any trees? Lucille wondered. But Mr. McDuffy's attention had moved on to other, more promising students. She fanned herself with her hand and began to unbutton her father's shirt. Mr. McDuffy noticed what she was doing and nervously pulled down the map of Texas and began to trace Coronado's route north from Mexico, thumping the map with the wooden yardstick he used for a pointer. Lucille knew he wouldn't look at her again before the class was over.

The Spanish explorers pulled their Chevies off the road and opened the trunks and got out a bunch of stakes with signs on them:

THIS WAY TO THE CITIES OF GOLD!
⎯⎯→

Coronado, who looked just like Julio Romero, pounded a stake into the ground with the back of a shovel, working up a fine sweat as he did it, pounding and pounding and pounding while the traffic drove by on the highway beside him, and Lucille Wintergarten in her grandmother's yellow Ford with only 22,000 miles on it drove past with the windows down and the Grateful Dead playing loud on the tape deck and the wind blowing through her ash-blonde hair.

6

Leon Stoner

Leon first met Lucille one Thursday evening about the time of year when the bravest farmers were planting their cotton, which is to say in early spring. He was sitting in the Gold Key liquor store, which he owned, staring at an old windmill in the field across the road, watching it disappear in the dusk and thinking about how the colors change when the light gets dim, when a car drove up and stopped beside the door, and the driver, a woman, got out. When she came in, Leon saw she was more a girl than a woman, maybe eighteen years old. Just inside the door she stopped and studied the sign on a display of Old Kentucky Home bourbon he'd set up just that morning. He studied her.

"Unless you're selling Girl Scout cookies, you're in the wrong place. You've got to be twenty-one to come in here."

Putting down the bottle she'd picked up, she turned a pair of big green eyes on him and said, "I *am* twenty-one. Just had my twenty-first birthday. I've got a driver's license to prove it."

Leon smiled and shook his head. He'd heard that one before.

She reached into the hip pocket of her jeans and hauled

out a wallet and snapped it open and flipped through it. "Here," she said, pulling something out. "Look at this." And she marched up to the counter and slapped down a driver's license and pointed at it with a chewed red fingernail.

Leon eyeballed it over his glasses, not bothering even to pick it up. It said her name was Lucille Marie Wintergarten, and according to the birth date shown she had been twenty-one for less than a week. But he could see where the old date had been scratched off with a razor blade and a new one typed in. The type didn't even match. He glanced from the driver's license back up to the girl's face—she smiled and showed a row of teeth as perfect as the keys of an accordion—and then back down at the license again.

"That's the worst forgery I've seen in nearly a year. Wha'd you do, make it yourself?"

Her eyebrows shot up. "It's *not* a forgery. I'm twenty-one and you've got to sell me whatever I want. That's the law."

Leon chuckled. "Well, listen here, Lucille Marie Wintergarten, maybe we oughtta call a cop and ask him about that."

She scowled.

He laughed out loud.

She picked up the driver's license and looked at it. "Is it really that bad?" she asked, holding it at a little distance like it was a painting and looking at it as if she'd never seen it before.

"Pretty bad. Might work someplace dark, if whoever you showed it to couldn't get a good look at you, but not here. How old are you anyway, about eighteen?"

"Almost," she said sadly, and put on a pout that was beautiful and silly at the same time. "How old are you?"

"Almost thirty-six," Leon said, and smiled. "You wouldn't want Old Kentucky Home anyway. That stuff would kill you."

"I've had bourbon before," she said defensively.

"Not that stuff, you haven't. It's like a tonsillectomy in a bottle. I wouldn't drink it."

"Well, what should I get?" she asked, pretending to look around the store but sliding her eyes around to look at him out of the corners.

She was wearing enough makeup for the whole cast of the Ice Capades, but under it her skin was smooth as cream. And her hair, beneath the metallic dye job, was long and thick. Over each of her eyes she had a smear of eye shadow the color of a parrot's wing. All in all, she was as raw and startling as a big mouthful of Old Kentucky Home.

"What should you *get*?" Leon said. "You should *get* a cherry lime and an order of french fries. You should *get* your homework done and *get* to bed early. You should probably *get* a lot of things, but you're too young to *get* anything from me. If I sold it to you, we'd both *get* in a lot of trouble. *Get* it?"

She tried to stop herself from smiling by putting on a terrible scowl, but it didn't work, at least not completely, and she shoved her driver's license back into her wallet and jammed it back into her hip pocket, although the way her jeans fit, Leon couldn't see how she'd managed it. He found himself smiling at her.

She marched over to a rack of cheap wine and picked up a bottle of something called Sweet Red Grape. "I've had this. It's good. What do you think?"

"I think it tastes like baby laxative. Only winos and kids drink it."

"Well, what *do* you like? You sell this stuff, you must like something."

Leon stood up off his stool and walked around from behind the little counter. What the hell am I doing? he thought. He went to a rack of wine and picked up a bottle of good vintage zinfandel. "I like this. It's the only wine I know of that you can drink with bar-b-q ribs." He handed it to her and she examined the label as if it were in code. He kept moving and picked up a bottle of W.L. Weller bourbon. "And I like this." He sloshed it and then put it back in place. She set down the wine and went over and picked up the bottle of bourbon to look at it. "And this is nice, if you like tequila," he said, touching a tall brown bottle as he walked by. "And that," he went on, pointing at a bottle of Pernod as he passed it, "is nice sometimes in the summer. And this stuff is the best rum you can get around here. And this is a good dry sherry. And that Baileys there is my favorite sweet drink. And this . . ." he'd worked his way, pointing out his choices as he went, quickly down one aisle and back up the other until he stood next to the beer coolers beside the cash register again, ". . . is the only beer I drink," he said, pointing at a bottle of Mackesons, "unless it's real hot, and then I drink Lone Star." He took one more step and was back behind the counter, where he'd been when she came in. "That's what I like. Some of what I like," he said, seating himself on the stool again.

"You've *tried* all this stuff?" she asked, looking around the shop in amazement.

"Not all at once."

She looked at him and smiled and leaned on the counter so that her breasts rested on her forearms, emphasizing what little cleavage she had. "So. Which do you think I should get?"

At that moment headlights swept across the windows as a car pulled up in the parking lot and stopped. Leon recognized it as belonging to the sheriff.

"Oh, shit. Quick. Get back here," he said, grabbing Lucille by the arm and pushing her through the door that led to the stockroom. She resisted, then realized what was happening and went quietly. By the time the sheriff had covered the fifteen feet to the door, she was out of sight and Leon was leaning on the counter, looking tense but okay.

"Evening, Sheriff."

"Evening."

The sheriff looked at the whiskey display, then wandered back to the cooler and took out a six of Pearl with each hand and set them on the counter.

"That it?" Leon asked.

"Yup."

When he was gone, Leon pushed through the stockroom door and found Lucille sitting on a case of wine drinking a can of Budweiser.

"He's gone. Now you better get out of here before somebody else shows up."

She smiled and leaned her head back and drained the last of the beer, holding the can a foot above her upturned mouth to drip the final drops onto her extended tongue.

"Come on," he said. "Get moving."

She put the can down and followed him back into the shop.

"But I still want something to drink."

"You just had something to drink. More'n you're supposed to. Come back when you're twenty-one. I can't sell you anything till then."

"But you already broke the law. You hid me back there and I drank a beer. You may as well sell me something now. Crime's already been committed."

He looked at her for a moment, then said, "What do you want from me?"

She looked around the shop and then went to the dessert drinks and picked up a bottle of Baileys Irish Cream. "This is the one you like, isn't it? Sweet, right?"

He didn't answer.

She brought it back to the counter and set it down with a thump and smiled.

"I told you, I can't sell you anything. You're not old enough." He was looking out the window at nothing again.

"Okay," she said. "How about I trade you for it?"

Suddenly she didn't seem so young; suddenly young had

nothing to do with it. She stretched across the counter and kissed him lightly but not too briefly right on the lips, staring into his eyes the whole time.

"How about that?" she said. There was no smile, but there was a glimmer of humor in her eyes.

"Get out of here."

"See you later," she said. And she took the bottle and left.

Leon knew a lot of women, sometimes he felt like he'd known too many. He often thought of his life as being marked off in epochs, divided by the different women he'd known: before Sharon Morrisson, after Sheila Wilks, between Cheryl Crosby and Mary Sue Bowling, the list went on and on, the past two decades being pretty finely divided this way among a long succession of schoolteachers, secretaries, cowgirls, coeds, nurses, fry cooks, cashiers, divorcées, debutantes, file clerks, bookkeepers, truck-stop waitresses, runway models, dental hygienists, bit-part actresses, airline stewardesses, and one frustrated housewife. But he did not consider himself either a chump or a total rakehell because of this, so as he watched Lucille Marie Wintergarten's car's taillights move away down the two-lane toward Tyrone he decided that the next time he ran into her he'd pay closer attention and try to keep things under control a little better.

The next time he ran into her it was late on a Friday night when summer was well on its way. The usual liquor-store crowd had come and gone, people heading home from work, picking up a few beers for the weekend, or going to a bar-b-q, dropping in for something to wash it down with. Leon's father had told him when he bought the Gold Key that "hard liquor sells when the sun shines, soft stuff sells after dark," and it had mostly proven to be true. Now it was midnight, the road outside was dark, and not even the beer was selling. Leon was reading a magazine when he heard the rattle of gravel in the parking lot and looked up to see a yellow car made dark gray by the vapor light, coming to a shuddering halt at the corner of the building. The car door opened and he recognized the girl.

When she came inside, he put away his magazine and watched her, waiting for her to say something.

"Hi, Leon. I know your name."

"It's no secret."

"I heard my aunt say something about you once."

"Who's your aunt?"

"Lucinda Ghertz. Know her?"

Leon nodded and groaned silently, thinking of the night he'd picked Lucinda up in Bigger 'n Dallas and how they'd stumbled out together at closing time, both drunk, and how he woke up beside her in the morning and lay there, hung over, trying to figure out how to get away without waking her.

"She moved away. You know that? Hey, that Baileys I got last time sure was good," she said.

"Yeah, I heard she'd left town."

"But the weather's getting so hot now, I think I'd like to try something that's not so sweet. You know, something refreshing. Got any suggestions?"

"Iced tea?"

She came over to the counter and leaned on it again and smiled up at him. "I heard you used to live in Europe. That right?"

"Yeah."

"How come you don't sound foreign?"

"I only lived in Europe for five years after high school. I was born and raised right here. Where'd you hear about all this?"

"Oh, I know a lot about you, Leon. I hear things all over, you know."

"Look, kid . . . Lucille . . . it's late and I'm tired. You've got no business in here. I'm about to close up."

"What were you doing in Europe?"

"I was in school part of the time. Then . . . I don't know. Just living."

"I bet you learned lots of things there. I hear Europe's real nice. And old. All those castles and things." She'd wandered over to a shelf of half-pints and was fiddling with them, looking at them as if they were toys.

"What are you doing? You know you can't buy anything; you know you're not supposed to be in here. What are you here for?"

"Here for? I just like to talk to you, Leon. You must know lots of interesting things, and I feel like I don't know anything. About fine wine. About the world. About . . . you know, anything. I just thought if I talked to you, I'd learn something." She looked at him out of her deep-green eyes. He couldn't read her expression, so he got up and started straightening things on the counter, taking the money out of the cash register, getting ready to go home.

"Why'd you go to Europe?" she asked, watching him count the money.

"I thought I could be an artist."

"Why'd you come back here? Why didn't you stay over there?"

"My mother was sick. And I was broke. I was working in a bookstore in Paris and I was tired of it and tired of having to think in two languages all the time."

"Wow! Paris! Is Paris nice? You speak French?"

"Not enough. Paris is okay," Leon said.

"Okay? That's all?"

He finished counting the money and stuffed it into a bank bag and looked up at her. "Paris is beautiful. That what you want me to say? It's even more beautiful than you've heard. It's unbelievably old and there are lots of trees and the streets are dirty and crooked and jammed with people from all over the world and there is so much art there that if I'd stayed the rest of my life I couldn't have looked at all of it. That's what a lot of Europe is like. But especially Paris." He zipped up the bank bag and closed the register.

"That sounds great! I wish I could see all that stuff. I'm gonna go someday." Then a peculiar hungry look came into her eyes and she said softer, "I sure wish I knew something about art and culture and all that. They didn't teach any of that where I went to school."

"I went to Tyrone High, same as you."

"Yeah. But you went *lots* earlier." She laughed.

Leon reached back through the stockroom door and threw the light switches, darkening the store and the sign outside so that the only light came from the burglar-alarm box and the moon and occasional passing cars. "Time for me to go home," he said, heading toward the front door.

"Where do you live?"

"North of town."

"Will you teach me about art and wine and all that? About Europe maybe? I'm pretty smart."

"You're too damn smart, and I'm not a teacher. I run a liquor store. And you've got no business being here."

"I don't mean teach me like a teacher. I just mean talk to me about it. Tell me what it's like. You already told me more about Paris than I knew before. Maybe I could come by sometime and we could talk. Maybe you could draw a picture of me. Don't you want me for a friend?"

They were at the door; Leon was holding it open for her. She stopped halfway through it and looked up at him from close range. Close enough that he could smell her and feel her breath. In the dim light her eyes looked very dark.

"Go," he said, and pushed her on through the door with his hand on her shoulder. "I don't want to talk about Europe." He locked the door. "And I quit art school because I wasn't good enough."

"You'd be good enough for me. And you like talking about

Europe. I can tell. What's the matter? You scared of me, Leon?"

"Ha!"

"Okay, we got some good steaks in the freezer at home. I'll come to your place on Tuesday when you're closed and we can cook 'em and talk about things."

She got in her car and slammed the door. He turned to say something, but the engine was cranking and then the motor revved, the headlights came on, and she fishtailed across the parking lot toward the road. As her car climbed up onto the blacktop he heard her yell back, "See you Tuesday. This time I'm trying the bourbon." And as she went by he saw that she was waving a stolen half-pint bottle at him and laughing.

"Jesus," he said, but he was laughing too.

The windmill across the road creaked rhythmically in the spring breeze.

"So how come you don't paint?"

"I like drawing better," Leon said distractedly. "A painting's too much. Too many things happening. A drawing's cleaner. No tricks. No place to hide."

Lucille was sprawled sideways in an old butterfly chair on the porch. The late summer's evening light shaded her but seemed to make her shine too, so that the contrast of her skin against the dark canvas of the chair was stark. Leon was looking intently back and forth from her to the drawing in his lap, trying to correct the angle of her leg.

"Did you move your knee?"

"My foot was going numb."

"Dammit, you're the one who wanted me to draw you. I can't do it if you keep moving around."

"Oh, Leon," she laughed and took another sip of wine.

The angle of her leg still looked awkward, and the pencil felt as clumsy as a fireplace poker, and the paper seemed to resist every mark he tried to make except those he made by mistake.

"You know Ronney?" she asked.

"Ronney? That crazy mechanic who comes in the shop?"

"I don't think he's so crazy. You know he was in Vietnam?"

"Um-hm. Saw him get up and make a speech about it one night out at Bigger 'n Dallas. Drunk as a skunk. Be still. Put your head back where you had it."

"I'm tired of this, Leon. Besides, I'm hungry."

"Don't move." But Lucille had already turned and was getting up to see what he'd done.

"Oh, that's so good," she said. "Do I really look like that?"

"Approximately."

"Can I have it?"

"If you want it. I do them for you."

"Sure I want it." She took the pad and looked at it for another minute, then sat down in his lap and put her arms around his neck and kissed him. "It's just like . . . ," she thought for a moment, then came up with the name, ". . . Degas," she said, and kissed him again, longer this time, taking his glasses off and running her fingers through his hair. "Thanks, Leon. I never had such a good drawing of myself before. Now can we eat?"

Leon felt the slip when it happened, the slide from knowing what he was doing to knowing he didn't care. It was like the shock and release a climber must feel when the rock gives way under his feet. Maybe it was that he wasn't sure what he wanted, or that what he wanted didn't make sense. Or maybe it was that Lucille *always* knew what she wanted, like a natural force, like gravity. He was swept up in her plans like a paper cup being sucked into the wake of a speeding cement truck, doing things he didn't want to do, going places he didn't want to go, and telling things he wanted to keep secret, till he felt as if he'd given her not only the keys to his house (which he had) but the keys to his life also, and now she was driving it as heedlessly as she drove her old yellow car. And the funny thing was, he didn't even care. As he finally realized one night, he had fallen in love with Lucille Marie Wintergarten. Fallen and fallen and fallen . . .

"Lucille?"

No answer, only a squirm.

Outside the bedroom windows the zing of cicadas had been replaced by the quieter rasp of crickets. The moon had risen two hours earlier and crept slowly up the screen till it was out of sight, but its light still sat on the windowsill like fine frost. On the highway a mile away two big semis tooted their horns at each other like animals calling. He looked down across Lucille's dozing form beside him.

"You awake?" he said softly.

"Mmmm."

"Will you marry me?" His voice when he said this seemed to come from somewhere just outside his head. He listened to it, amazed and thrilled and horrified at what it was saying.

"Mmmm . . . What?"

"I love you, Lucille," his voice said, still on its own.

For a moment she didn't move or breathe. Then she pushed herself up onto her elbow and looked at him, and finally sat back away from him and looked again. The pale light from the window painted a rim of silvery gray down one side of her, and he marveled at the texture of her skin. She pushed her hair back with one hand and rubbed her eyes.

"What did you say?" Her speech was blurred with sleep.

Leon didn't say anything. He breathed deeply.

She said, "I don't love you, Leon. Not that way. We're just friends. I, I don't want to marry anybody. Not now. Not yet."

He swallowed, grateful for the dark. "I knew that. I was

just . . . kidding. Testing. To see if you were paying attention." Now it was his regular voice, shaping each word carefully in his mouth. After a moment he swallowed and stretched and said, "It's after midnight. You better be heading home, hadn't you?" listening to be sure he didn't waver.

"Yeah, I guess I better."

"Hey, Lucille. This is Leon. I just thought I'd call you up and see if you wanted to come by later. It's been a slow night, and I was thinking of closing early. I've got a couple of lobsters at the house. You ever eat a lobster?"

"Thanks, Leon, but I can't." She sounded far away, even though it was only a local call. Outside the window a tractor went by pulling a trailer-load of cotton edged pink by the sunset. "My car's got a problem and I dropped it off with Ronney earlier to get it fixed. I told him I'd come by and talk to him about it tonight."

"How about after that? I'm not in a big hurry, and the lobsters are dead, so they'll wait."

"Mmmm . . . I don't think so. Thanks anyway."

"Okay. Maybe another time."

"Maybe." *Click.*

He hung up slowly, watching the phone come to rest in its cradle. There were no lobsters in the freezer. He didn't have anything at all to eat at home. But if she'd accepted, he'd have happily driven up to Lubbock and bought lobsters or any other damn thing she wanted. Only he'd been pretty sure she wouldn't before he called.

Out front a station wagon pulling a long dirty horse trailer swung unsteadily off the road into the parking lot and stopped—some drunk shitkicker coming in for another bottle. Leon settled his chin in his hand and looked out at the old windmill spinning against the red autumn clouds and tried to think of Paris and the light above the Seine.

7

Roy Stoner

I guess as a person gets older the circle around 'em draws in closer and closer, like a target disappearin' down to the bull's-eye. Now it's down to just me. Leon comes once or twice a week. But mostly it's just me and the TV set. I go out sometimes. I do my shoppin' and get the oil changed in the car ever' thousand miles and keep the lawn mowed in the summer. But I don't see people much anymore. Not people I know.

When I was little, there was Mom, Dad, Earl and Elmer, Aunt Bett, and me. Mealtime was so noisy you'd'a thought we were three times that many. Those twins were always gettin' into somethin'—play-fightin', doin' tricks on one another, jokin' around all the time. They were fourteen years older than me, so they were already big boys when I first remember them. I used to wonder if I'd ever be as big as they were. By the time I started school they were already out workin', but they both lived at home till they were past twenty-one. When they finally moved away, mealtime got a lot quieter—just Mom and Dad and Aunt Bett and me. Except on Sundays, when my brothers came to dinner.

They lived together in a little frame house down behind

where the forge used to be before it was torn down for the Dairy Queen. Elmer would work in the forge all day and Earl would go out and work on windmills, Aermotors mostly, although there were still a couple of old Stars around then. Sometimes he needed special parts and Elmer would make 'em for him. I would go after school and sit out in the forge on a keg o' nails an' talk to Elmer while he worked. Once in a while I'd pump the bellows for him, and he'd always be pushin' me: "Come on, you little pismire, pump, pump, pump, pump!" he'd yell, yellin' me on, and I'd go at it till my muscles were so tired I could hardly walk home for dinner. I loved to watch Elmer work, the way he handled the horses that came in for shoein', and how he shaped the hot iron.

I liked Earl just as well, though. Once or twice he took me out to see what he did. He had come home early a few times and found me sittin' and talkin' to Elmer and finally he asked me, "You want to come out to Tarbuckle's big windmill with me sometime?" It was like he was tryin' to top Elmer and show me somethin' better. Tarbuckle still had one of the great big old windmills—an old Eclipse. Well, I went with him okay, but I was afraid to climb to the top. Once on a smaller windmill he managed to get me to climb all the way up to the platform. But it scared me, even though he was right there holdin' on to me. Goin' with Earl wasn't as much fun as bein' in the forge with Elmer. For two men who seemed so alike, they sure were different to be at work with. Earl was all air and wind and sunshine. Elmer was smoke and the heat from the fire. Earl was spinnin' blades and cold gushin' water. Elmer was nervous horses and big hammers.

When Earl was twenty-six, he fell off a windmill he was workin' on and broke his right arm at the elbow. Three months later Elmer got kicked by Harvey Woodlock's big white mule and got his left arm broke, also at the elbow. If both o' them had had their arms broke at the same time they'da looked like a pair of bookends. It was a good thing that didn't happen, though. Neither of 'em could work with a broken arm, so while each twin was laid up, the other had to make enough money to keep 'em both goin'.

Neither one of 'em ever got married, although they both fell in love with the same woman. It happened right after Aunt Bett got sick, the sickness she 'ventually died from. Mom had thought a professional nurse might help her get better, like she was blamin' herself for not nursin' the old woman good enough, same way she blamed herself for a lot o' things that had nothin' whatever to do with her. Anyway, she heard about a girl in Wilson who had just graduated from the nursin' school at Scott and White Hospital. This girl, whose name was Dolores, had come home to help her mother, who was a partial invalid. She was livin' with her and workin' for a young doctor named Dr. O'Banion.

Times were hard around Wilson. The railroad had just closed the spur that went through there. Dr. O'Banion couldn't keep Dolores on but part-time. So Mom got in touch with her, and she started comin' over twice a week to see Aunt Bett. That was how my brothers met her.

Earl was the first, like he was at most things. He dropped by the house one day to get somethin' to eat on his way back from a job. It must have been either a Tuesday or a Friday because those were Dolores's days. Anyway, from the first minute he saw her he was in love with her. He had an old Ford pickup that he used in his work, and he offered to give her a ride back to Wilson that day. She accepted.

I don't know if Elmer heard about Dolores from Earl or not. He might o' heard about her from Mom and Dad. But the next time she came to see Aunt Bett he made it a point to come by the house and meet her. The way Mom told the story, when Dolores first met him she thought he was Earl, since they looked so much alike, an' she started talkin' to him real friendly. Like she already knew him. Elmer played her along, not lettin' on, till she finally realized somethin' was goin' on. The twins looked so much alike that a person who didn't know them could easy enough make that mistake.

I was only about thirteen when Dolores was around, but I remember her quite well. She wasn't very big, but she had a way of movin' and talkin' that made her seem bigger than she was. Maybe it was because she was a nurse and was used to bein' in charge o' things. She also had a way of lookin' at you that made you think she was prettier than she really was. Years later, after Elmer died, I found a photograph of her in his things. I was surprised how plain she was. Not ugly by any means, just kinda plain and regular-lookin', nothin' special. But when you were around her, she seemed real pretty. Both my brothers thought she was the prettiest thing they'd ever seen.

There got to be a real rivalry between them over her, the same way there'd been over all sorts of things—over havin' me help 'em work, or, when they were still at home, over which one of 'em had to sleep in the top bunk, or over who could run faster or shoot better or throw a baseball the farthest. Earl would drop by and see her in Wilson if he had work on a windmill anywhere out that way. Sometimes he'd drive miles out of his way to get there and pretend like he just happened to be in the neighborhood. Elmer would take her for rides on the weekend in a little buggy he had that was pulled by a buckskin mare named Elsie.

It didn't take long for the competition between them to get pretty hot. Got where some days I'd go over to their house and they'd hardly be speakin' to one another. It probably would have been okay if Dolores had made a choice between them. A man can take losin' better than he can take not knowin'. But maybe, 'cause they were twins and so much alike, she couldn't make up her mind. Or maybe she just liked havin' 'em compete for her. Some people are like that.

Anyway, she didn't choose. The competition went on for most of a year, each brother tryin' to beat the other and the atmosphere between 'em gettin' worse and worse.

Finally Aunt Bett died, as everybody had known she would. And Dolores quit comin' to the house. That meant the twins had to go to Wilson to see her. This gave Earl a clear advantage, because he had the Ford, which was better for that distance than Elmer's buggy.

But one Saturday when he was supposed to go see Dolores, his Ford broke down. There was a crack in the oil pan where he'd high-centered on a rock, as I recall. Somehow he got back to town without knowin' about it. Anyway, after he'd changed clothes and came out to start it again, so he could go call on Dolores, it pumped a big puddle of oil out on the ground and began makin' all kinds o' noise. Well, he shut it off and took off his good coat and lay down on his back and slid under to have a look at what the matter was. I remember watchin' him there with his legs stuck out from under the pickup. And I remember how he cussed when he saw that crack where the oil was comin' out. It shouldn't have really been a serious problem. A blacksmith could have fixed it in a few minutes. It was a simple enough job to put a patch on. And soon as it was patched, the car would be fine. If things had been different, Elmer would have dropped everything and had that oil pan patched in no time. The forge was already hot. But Earl wouldn' ask him. And Elmer wouldn' volunteer. So the solution wasn't as simple as it should have been.

I remember Earl standin' there beside that truck with his sleeves rolled up, lookin' from that puddle of oil to everything in the world but the forge. Elmer was in the forge makin' a weather vane in the shape of a milk cow. Just playin', really, since the weather vane was only for himself. I know he could hear Earl cussin' that Ford. And in his cussin', Earl mentioned several times exactly what was wrong.

"Damn that cracked oil pan," he said, loud enough so his brother and anybody else in the neighborhood who wasn't deaf could hear. But neither man would budge. They both just kept doin' what they were doin'—Earl cussin' and Elmer playin' with his milk-cow weather vane and the whole situation heatin' up like a flatiron.

It crossed my mind to go ask Elmer to come fix the oil pan. He'da done it if I'd asked. But I couldn't. It would've been like takin' sides against him.

After a while, he got tired o' playin' with the weather vane. He quenched it and doused the fire and put up his tools real careful and went in the house. After a few minutes, he came out and walked into town with his hands in his pockets, not lookin' around at all, just leavin' Earl there with his broken Ford and me watchin' both of them, wishin' I wasn't but afraid to leave.

A few weeks after that, Earl moved into his own house. It was a little place near where the old railroad station used to be, about as far from Elmer's as he could get and still be in Tyrone.

In the end, things didn't work out for Elmer either. Dolores married Dr. O'Banion. But as far as my brothers were concerned, the damage was done. They stayed civil to each other. They sat next to one another when they came home for Sunday dinner. They talked and were pleasant so long as somebody else was around, and when I visited one of them he would always ask me about the other first thing. But that was it. They never visited each other's house nor got together in any way on their own.

Years and years later, after I was grown and finally married, I told all this to Ruth. We made it a point of always havin' 'em over at the same time. But it was no good. When that oil pan cracked, it was like their twinship cracked with it. By the time we started tryin' to patch it, they'd buried the argument so far down in their guts there probably wasn't anything that could have gotten it out. At Dad's funeral, and then two years later at Mom's, they stood side by side, still lookin' just alike, even dressed similar, but they didn't talk much. It was like they couldn't, like they'd forgot the language.

When Leon was born, I wanted to name him Elmer Earl Stoner, after both of 'em, thinkin' that bein' together in the name of a nephew might do some good. Besides, they were my brothers. But Ruth didn't like the sound of it. She pointed out that we'd have to decide whether it would be Elmer Earl or Earl Elmer, and whichever way we went might bother the one who came second. Besides, she wanted to name him after her father, so we did that: Leon. No middle name.

Earl died first. Since he was workin' alone, nobody was sure how it happened. One day Mr. Godley decided he'd go out and see how Earl was comin' along replacin' the blades on the old windmill on his south forty, that had broke off in a sandstorm. When he got there, he found Earl all crumpled up next to the base. The coroner said from the way he was busted up he must have fallen all the way from the top. He had no business bein' a windmill monkey at his age. He was seventy.

Earl's death hit all of us hard. Even Ruth. I remember Leon cried and cried 'cause that was the first person he ever knew who died. But it hit Elmer hardest. I was the one who had to tell him. He was in the forge, like he always was, makin' horseshoes and tossin' 'em over in a pile in the corner. On the way over there, I decided that the best thing would be to tell him straight-out, so I did. "Elmer," I said, havin' to yell over the noise of his hammer and the deafness he'd got over the years, "Elmer, I got some real bad news." He glanced up but just kept beatin', like nothin' I could tell him could be as important as that horseshoe he was makin'. "It's about Earl," I said. He just kept beatin'. It made me kinda' mad, the way he was ignorin' me. I yelled out, "He fell off Mr. Godley's big windmill. He's dead." And then he stopped, holdin' the hammer up over his head like he was suddenly turned into a statue of himself, still lookin' down at that half-made horseshoe on the anvil, watchin' as the color went out of it.

He never was right after that. It was hard to put your finger on what was the matter with him, but it was like he developed a slow leak or something. He seemed to gradually go limp. He kept gettin' up every day and goin' into the forge and makin' horseshoes, but even that was a kind of sign of what was wrong. There were no horses anymore. Hadn't been for years, 'cept for a few pets and some rodeo stock. But he went on poundin' iron the same as he had all his life, like he was a machine somebody'd gone off and left runnin'. The blacksmith business was over and he was an old man and should have been retired, but he still kept at it, beatin' them out—shoes for draft horses, shoes for little ponies, shoes for horses with hoof problems, and shoes for horses that had to walk on slick roads, all of them long since dead and gone. But he kept poundin' their shoes out and tossin' 'em over into a big pile in a corner of the forge. It was like he was expectin' every horse that ever lived to come back to life someday, like those Indians, the Ghost Dancers, who were always waitin' for the buffalo to return and everything to go back the way it had been. But the streets were full of Chryslers and Fords and Chevies now, and the bing-bing-bing from the forge was just pure craziness and everybody knew it. But maybe he didn't know what else to do. Anyway, that next December the paperboy found him one mornin', draped across his own anvil like he was waitin' to be beat into some new shape himself. He'd been dead since sometime the previous evenin', according to the doctor. Or maybe part of him had been dead since March, when Earl fell off o' that windmill, 'cause ever since then it'd been like he was just waitin' to follow, like him and Earl had been racin' to some goal and he was hurryin' to catch up, just drivin' himself along with his hammer. There were over a thousand horseshoes in the corner of the forge when he died. I counted 'em.

Christmas dinner that year I was so lonesome.... There was just me and Ruth and Leon at the table, and I couldn't stop thinkin' about all the people that weren't there anymore—Elmer and Earl, Mom and Dad, Aunt Bett. Maybe bein' the baby of the family made me like that. I don't know. I just hate bein' alone, though. If it'd been up to me, I'd've had ten kids. I think part of the reason I married Ruth, who was so much younger than myself, was because I thought we'd do that. But she had different ideas. She wouldn't go for it atall, even though we'd talked about it beforehand. I can't really blame her. She had a hard time havin' Leon: sick all the time and a bad delivery. But a man and a woman with only one child is no real family.

Just before Leon graduated high school he came to me one day and told me he wanted to go to college in Europe. I thought he was kiddin' at first. He didn't know anybody in Europe. But he had this idea in his head that Europe was where the art was, and art was what he thought he wanted to do. I tried to talk him out of it, but he didn't pay me any attention. Ruth wouldn' even try to talk him out of it. She said since we could afford it we oughta let him go. I never thought she cared about him the way mothers ought to care about their children, 'specially when they've got only one. Since he wanted to go and she wanted him to go, there was no way I could talk him out of it. So the end of that summer he left. Then it was just me and Ruth. I moved the extra dinin'-room chairs up to the attic.

After he was gone, the house was so quiet we could practically hear one another think. I used to sneak into the other room and call him up sometimes in the middle of the night, when it was already mornin' over there, just to hear him talk.

We never had much to say to each other, but I just wanted to hear him. Sometimes in the evenin's, when me and Ruth were sittin' around, me readin' or watchin' TV and her workin' on one of those big jigsaw puzzles, she'd say, "Idn' it nice and quiet?" And it was quiet all right. Quiet as the grave. I started keepin' the store open extra hours just to be around people and away from so much quiet.

Leon stayed in Europe till Ruth had her heart attack. Five years. When he came back, he was hardly himself anymore. Same face and all, but he talked different and he dressed different and he acted different. He was older, but so were we. Ruth wasn't near as old as me, but she might as well have been, the way her body was givin' out on her. Ever' time I went to the hospital she seemed worse than before. Her face had started agin' real fast, and ever' time I left the hospital it seemed like before I could get back, a little part of the woman I married would be replaced by part of a sickly old . . . When she was asleep, which was a lot of the time, I'd sit there by her and watch her face, watchin' to see if I could catch the change goin' on. But I never saw it. I loved Ruth, God knows I did, but I got where I hated those changes—the way her eyes were sinkin' back in her head, the way the tendons in her neck began to stick out like guy wires. At the end I could hardly stand to look at her, 'cause what was left, that body in the bed, didn't seem like her at all. Just like some bad replacement. Like somebody had stole her away and put this scarecrow in her place.

She was pretty far gone when Leon got back, even though he came as quick as he could. I was afraid of what he'd say when he saw how she looked, but he didn't say anything. Maybe he'd been gone so long he'd forgotten how pretty she'd been. I don't know. But he didn't say anything.

She didn't last long after he came back. He and I were stayin' shifts with her so that when she went she wouldn't be alone, but that last day I was runnin' late because I'd fallen asleep in my reclinin' chair in the livin' room. I called and told him I was on my way. It was past dinnertime and he knew I'd be there any minute, so he went ahead and took off to go get a hamburger at the Dairy Queen. I got there about twenty minutes later 'cause I'd run to the Mini Mart to get a magazine to read. But when I got there, the nurses had already pulled the sheet up over her face. One of 'em had come in to check on her a few minutes after Leon left and found her dead. He said she'd been breathin' okay when he left. It was like she was waitin' to be alone to die, like there was something embarrassing or secret about it.

That night when I went home, I couldn't sleep. The quiet of the house was like water drownin' me. I sat in our bedroom and looked at old pictures for a long time, 'specially my favorite picture of her, tryin' to remember how she used to look so I could forget how bad she looked at the end. About two o'clock in the morning I went into the bathroom to pee and get a drink of water, and I looked in the mirror, the way you do sometimes, and I saw some of the same things that had happened to her—the eyes set way back and the neck tendons stickin' out and the skin like thin leather—in my own face. I nearly screamed. If Leon hadn't been around then, I don't know what I'da done. So I don't guess I should complain about the things he's gotten into since.

Soon as the funeral was over, I started figurin' how I could keep him here. He'd said how he wasn't makin' any money in Europe, so I decided to sell him the liquor store. I was old enough to be retired anyway, and if he had it he'd stay around town and he'd make some money. It wasn't like havin' the keys to Fort Knox, but it was a good business, and I could afford to sell it to him on credit.

So I got all the papers together and one evenin' I made him the offer. He sat there and looked at me like I was tryin' to sell him a car I'd been runnin' back the mileage on. Like I was tryin' to trick him somehow. Hell, if I'd wanted to, I coulda sold that place for lots more plenty of times. I'd had offers. But I didn't get mad. There was no point in that. He thought about it for a few days, and he finally took it, but he acted like he was doin' me a big favor.

Soon as we got the papers signed, he took Ruth's old car (which I'd told him he could have) and moved way out in the country. There was plenty of room in our house. I'd hoped he'd stay till he got married, but he wanted his own place.

For a while it looked like he might be gonna get married. He had a regular girlfriend, the Morrisson girl that he'd gone around with in high school. But she threw him over for a horse rancher. Cain't say I really blame her.

Now I only see him about once or twice a week. We go out for steaks maybe, or I get some bar-b-q and have him over. We sit and watch TV. Wrestlin' seems to be what we watch most, unless it's football season. Sometimes we talk about how the store's doin'. He asks my advice; then when I give it to him, he acts like I'm buttin' in. I'd like to talk to him about more important stuff, but we never get around to it.

I'm an old man now. I won't be around forever. When I'm gone, he won't have anybody atall 'less he shapes up. I want to tell him that. I want to tell him what it's like to not have anybody. But instead, we talk about football and the wrestlin' on TV and how the shop's doin'. He thinks I don't know about the things he does. But I know. I've heard how he's chasin' everything in skirts. How some of the women he hangs around with are married and some of them are just schoolgirls. And how it's somebody different every weekend. "Soon enough it'll be nobody, Leon," I want to say. "You better get somebody you can get along with and settle down. The clock's turnin'. The years are passin'. Look at me. I'm old and alone, but not as alone as you're gonna be." I wanna grab him and shake him and make him look up ahead and see what's comin', but I cain't figure out how to do it.

8

Sharon Ann Morrisson

The It'll Do Lounge was located on the edge of Neptune, which is like saying it was located on the edge of the world, since Neptune was just a little crossroads that anyone with a healthy arm could throw a rock across—a consolidated school with a drive-in burger joint across from it, a Shamrock gas station, a long-abandoned grocery store called Rose & Blacky's Quick Shop, and a few scattered houses. Not a real town at all. Nevertheless, the It'll Do wasn't even in the middle of this but was only on the edge, where people drove past it on the way to somewhere else, the Piggly Wiggly in Tyrone or the Purina store in O'Donnell or some other place that had nothing to do with the likes of the It'll Do Lounge except for an accident of geography. A country bar in a place as dry as the Texas panhandle is usually a landmark, but this one was a landmark only in the sense that a loose tread in a flight of stairs might be a landmark. There was only one class of people who went there on a regular basis. That was the class of those with something to hide, the class of people whose daily lives were like the lyrics of country-western songs: *"Pleeeeaaaaasse release meeeee, let me goooooo, 'cause IIIIIIII don't love youuuuuuu, inyyyyy mooooore."* People like that. They'd come to form the exclusive clientele of this little bar on the edge of the world, and over the years they'd turned it into a sort of elephants' graveyard of busted hearts and broken promises. The fellow who owned it, a guy named Reiley Woodlock, a failed milo farmer, had originally had it in his mind for the It'll Do to be a kind of exclusive cattlemen's club, a place for big deals to be struck in a haze of whiskey fumes and cigar smoke. But somehow it hadn't turned out that way. Right after the bar opened, a farmer's wife from Seagraves and a football player from Texas Tech began meeting there on the sly. Then one night the football player got shot when he went out to his car. And after that, the reputation of the place was made, and everybody knew that if you wanted someplace to meet somebody you weren't supposed to meet at all, the place you wanted was the It'll Do Lounge out on the edge of Neptune.

It was a strange place for a rendezvous: dim, as such places are supposed to be, but not the glowing candle-lit dim of a sexy cigarette advertisement. It was more a sort of downhearted dim, the dim of extinction and disappointment. Mr. Woodlock had realized as soon as the bar turned (that's the way he put it, like it had gone bad the same way a bottle of milk sours—"The place turned right after that college kid got shot," he'd say bitterly) that he wasn't going to make a lot of money out of the place. People with something big on their conscience usually want to drown it in the cheapest available liquid. They say, "I'll have a double shot of Old Kentucky Home." Never, "I'll have a bottle of Dom Pérignon." So, because he didn't sell a lot of the high-priced stuff, he decided he'd better cut his overhead if he was going to survive. As a result, the only illumination in the It'll Do came from a nineteen-inch black-and-white TV, the lights on the cigarette machine, a few neon beer signs the distributors had put up around the room, and one bare fluorescent tube that hung down like a trapeze over the cash register. There was also a jukebox, an old Wurlitzer with bubbles ascending through colored liquid on each side of a stack of 45s of the kind of music written about the kind of people who hung out in places like the It'll Do Lounge, and it played all the time. It was almost as if the bar had its own sound track. There wasn't a week go by that some disheartened drunk didn't say, "I be a son of a bitch. That song sounds jis like what happen' to me," and then order a fresh one of whatever he was drinking in celebration of the fact. Or maybe a covert couple in the gloom of the back booth would nudge each other over some sappy piece of music as if to say, "Our song."

Because the jukebox was always going, the sound on the TV was never turned up except for from eight to nine on Sunday nights, when Mr. Woodlock would unplug the jukebox so he could watch *Bonanza*. Other than that, the TV's sole function seemed to be to cast its shifting spectral glow over the customers. And because it was used this way and was worked all the time, its picture eventually began to roll and grow fuzzy, so that the Sunday-night episodes of *Bonanza* became increasingly confused:

"Is that Hoss?"

"Naw, that's Adam."

"Cain't be Adam. He always wears black, like Paladin. 'Sides that, he ain't been around for years."

"Yeah, well, it ain't big enough for Hoss. Maybe it's Sheriff Coffee."

But nobody could tell for sure. The picture tube was too far gone. Finally Mr. Woodlock took to bringing down a little twelve-inch Japanese portable on Sundays. He'd put it on the end of the bar and watch his show, then take it back home with him for the rest of the week. The old black-and-white set was relegated to the status of a navigational aid for those trying to find their way out of the bar. They knew it was by the door.

But this is not the story of the It'll Do Lounge, or even the story of Reiley Woodlock and how he went from inheriting a big farm to pouring beer behind the bar of a trashy little honky-tonk. This is the story of a woman named Sharon Morrisson and her boyfriend of four year's standing, whose name was Chuck Bonner.

Neither Sharon nor Chuck was the type you'd normally think to find in a place like the It'll Do Lounge. They were well-scrubbed, hardworking, honest, outdoorsy folks who shared a love of good horses, good sense, and each other. But since Chuck was a man and Sharon was a woman, there was still plenty of ground for misunderstanding left, even though they were apt to forget that fact sometimes.

Sharon and Chuck had first met about a dozen years earlier at a rodeo in Post, when she was twenty and he was twenty-three. She'd been there competing in the barrel racing, and Chuck was in the saddle-bronc event, which Sharon's second oldest brother, Charley, was in too. Charley introduced them and they talked for a few minutes before one of them had to go ride, but after that first meeting they didn't run into each other again for eight years because Chuck was traveling on the rodeo circuit. Then one Friday night Sharon was out at Bigger 'n Dallas with all three of her brothers, Charley and Leo (the oldest) and Morris, and Chuck happened to be there too. By this time he was living back near Tyrone, earning a living as a horse trader, and all that remained of his rodeo career was a permanent limp from the riding accident that had ended it. But it wasn't a bad limp, so he came over and asked Sharon to dance. She accepted. While they were dancing, he reminded her that they'd met before and told her where and when. It was only then that she recognized the face of the brave young bronc rider behind his weathered features and prematurely graying hair. He seemed to remember everything about their first meeting at that long-ago rodeo. He recalled, for instance, that she'd placed second on a roan gelding named Dandy.

"How do you remember all that stuff?" she asked, more flattered than she'd been in some time.

"Oh," he replied, smiling, "I never forget a horse."

They both laughed, and the band sang, *"I'm wawkin' the floor over you, I cain't sleep a wink it is true . . . ,"* and by the time the song was over they were going together. For a few weeks he was still seeing Rose Strong and she still went out some with Leon Stoner, but Chuck and Rose had a disagreement over something, and Sharon never could take Leon seriously, so it wasn't long before it was just Sharon and Chuck and Chuck and Sharon, like ham and eggs and salt and pepper.

Sharon Morrisson looked exactly like what she was: a secretary-bookkeeper in a cotton gin who rode horses every spare minute she could. She had a compact, strong body, a well-sculpted face that was always tan, brown eyes, and long chestnut hair that she kept braided and coiled on the back of her head unless she was dancing or making love to Chuck; then she took it down and it hung in a dark cascade on either side of her face. Because of the kind of life she lived, she almost always dressed in blue jeans and flat shoes and shirts, which suited her figure and were practical as well. She had, as mentioned before, three brothers, two older and one younger, and no sisters. Women raised in families where they are surrounded by men tend to fall into one of two categories: either they are spoiled rotten and convinced that men want to and are capable of looking after them, or they are independent-minded and harbor few illusions about the opposite sex, having seen it close-up throughout their formative years. Sharon fell into the second category. She could ride better than any of her brothers except Charley and outshoot any of them, and she thought nothing of standing toe-to-toe with a man in any argument. Her combination of competence and strong good looks had attracted a fair number of admirers through the years, but she was not a woman who was impressed by a man just because of his gender. So all those who came to her thinking they could suck up some of her strength were immediately rebuffed, and some of the others made too many demands. She'd been lonely sometimes, but that's often what strength costs. Not being a deep thinker, she hadn't pondered this, but her strength saw her through, so it didn't matter much in the end. And after she met Chuck, she knew the loneliness hadn't been in vain. He fit into her life like a foot into a custom-made boot. Sometimes, when they made love and he dozed off beside her, she would look at him and try to imagine what it would be like for them to be lying beside each other in twenty years. And in her imagination it was good. But she had just enough romance in her to want him to ask first. "Tell me, Chuck. Tell me you want me forever," she would say in her mind, like a person making a wish on a falling star.

One of the things Sharon and Chuck shared besides their love and their love of horses was a certain amount of contrariness. It probably wasn't much worse than most people's, but it was enough to get in the way now and then. For instance, about six inches ago Chuck had suggested that if Sharon cut her hair short it wouldn't be so much trouble for her in the mornings. She'd been toying with the idea of doing just that and had even asked him what he thought about it, but she didn't like the way he made his suggestion (he was standing outside the bathroom door one morning waiting for her to get out so he could get in), so she decided then and there that she'd have long hair forever. But more important than Sharon's hair was the question of marriage. They'd been going together for four years. They loved each other. Both of them had obviously thought about making it permanent. But one day, after Chuck had hurt his back falling off a young stallion he'd just bought, Sharon came out to see him, and half joking, she made some comment about how if he wasn't careful he'd end up as an old man living alone with his horses and nobody to look after him. And in the way a thing will sometimes remind a person of its opposite, he suddenly found himself thinking of all the good times he'd had before Sharon had come along, remembering how exciting life had been back then. It was not so much that he suddenly wanted to get away from her; he just found himself not wanting to get any closer, but the result was the same, since movement is the unavoidable requirement of life and all things not getting closer are getting farther apart.

This might have come to no more than a few weeks of grumpiness if fate hadn't provided a focus for what Chuck was feeling just then. But it did. The name of the focus was Martha Godley, formerly Martha Godley Simon but now just Martha Godley again, since she'd shed her husband before moving to Tyrone. Martha was a whole other kind of person from Sharon. She was rounder, paler, louder, taller, and had a completely different view of how life worked. Where Sharon thought of people as all moving along through life in more or less the same direction, like water going downstream, Martha thought of them as orbiting around her like planets around a star. She was lovely to look at, always had been, and she'd learned early to use her beauty to make herself the center of dramatic events. Drama made her feel bright and special. So everywhere she went, fights and conflicts seemed to break out around her like spontaneous combustion.

Martha had married Tom Simon, a disc jockey, when she was twenty, and they'd moved around from one place to another following his jobs—from Lubbock to Oklahoma City to Pueblo to Santa Fe—but everywhere they went trouble dogged them. Things always started out okay, but after they'd been someplace a while, something would always go wrong and Tom would find himself unable to get along with his boss or with the people he worked with. He could never figure out how it happened. Martha pointed out failings to him (and God knows there were plenty), but even when he corrected what she pointed out—bought nicer clothes, combed his hair differently, got a better car, or drank a better brand of liquor—there was always something wrong, always trouble.

Then finally Tom did something that got him pitched in jail—assault and battery, thirty days—and behind bars he finally got some time to think without Martha around to help him. As he lay in his cell one night it dawned on him that wherever they went things were always okay until his lovely wife got acquainted with the people he worked with. And that's when everything fell apart. Next morning Martha saw the dawning revelation in his face when she came to visit, but there was nothing she could do about it. He was not interested in her suggestions this time. So quick as he got out from behind bars, she told him she wanted a divorce. She had no desire to be married to a jailbird, she said.

Beaten to the punch and realizing he always had been and always would be, he gave her what she wanted, including most of their joint bank account and the Buick Skylark convertible they'd just purchased. Then he went on with his life and she went on with hers, driving back to the bosom of her family to look for fresh game.

Martha's mother's sister's husband, Martha's Uncle Willard, owned the western-wear shop in Tyrone, and it so happened that his assistant manager had just quit unexpectedly, leaving a job opening. Uncle Willard knew the value of having a pretty woman around to wait on the cowboys, so he was happy to hire Martha. About a month later, while she was rearranging the boots and Willard was off at the café drinking coffee with his buddies, Chuck Bonner came in to buy some jeans. Martha had noticed him around town and liked his looks and knew that he raised horses, so she asked him to explain the differences in the various saddles and bridles and blankets and bits the store stocked. Chuck hadn't been looking for her or even wishing for her, but now he took one look at her, with her blonde hair and blue eyes and big inviting smile, and saw her as a door swinging open, like an escape hatch. Another time he would have just smiled back and that would have been the end of it; he'd have seen her for what she was. But now he didn't really see her at all; he just saw a woman who was available and pretty and not Sharon Morrisson.

This is where the It'll Do Lounge comes into the story.

As part of his business, Chuck gave riding lessons, so people, more than half of them female, came and went from his place all the time. But as far as anything beyond business, anything that might involve their going indoors together, there was a need for another rendezvous if he wanted to be sure that Sharon didn't interrupt the proceedings. She had a key to his house and was prone to showing up unannounced. So one night a few weeks after Chuck and his ambivalence encountered Martha and her loneliness, the two of them found themselves sitting in the back booth of the It'll Do holding hands in the dark and sipping beers to the insistent whine of the jukebox. *"Stan' byyyy yuuuurrrr mannnnnnnnnnn . . . ,"* it bleated, and the snowy shapeless shadows on the old TV rolled like the dreams of a restless sleeper.

Chuck had told Sharon he was going up to Amarillo to talk to a man about rodeo business and wouldn't be back till late. He'd told her he'd call her the next day. Now, instead of being in Amarillo, he'd been here in the dark for an hour with another woman. Martha was telling him about her exhusband. She was saying how the man had been unstable and prone to violence and blamed her for everything and made her life a misery. When she got to the end of her sad tale, having landed herself in Tyrone, friendless and in need of comfort and company, she batted her long eyelashes and squeezed Chuck's fingers and said, "How about you, Chuck?

Surely a man as handsome as you must have somebody special in his life."

Suddenly Chuck found that he had come to a divergence in his path. He could tell her the truth: "Yep. I've got a girlfriend, who I love," but then he would have had to add, "but that doesn't mean I don't want to hang around with you too," and he knew that wouldn't fly. Not because it wasn't true, but because he was dealing with someone who wouldn't see things the way he did. And Martha hadn't asked the question for information anyway. She already knew all about Sharon. She'd asked to put him on the spot and make him choose. Now she leaned a little closer and looked up at him, trying to tilt the odds in her favor.

Chuck really wanted to be here with Martha. The alternative was that he'd lied to Sharon for nothing. And looking at Martha now, through the combined effects of three beers, the cloud of Chanel No. 5 that she emitted, and the songs from the jukebox, he wanted more than just to be here with her. He wanted to try her on for size and sample her for taste, grab her around her middle and feel his fingers on her back and do things to her that had nothing at all to do with love or having somebody special in his life or anything else except the pure biological expression of masculine feelings. So he squeezed her fingers back and said, "Oh, you know . . . I go out now and then . . . but there's nobody . . . really special," meaning only that there was nobody really special he wanted to talk about at this particular moment sitting here in the back booth of the notorious It'll Do Lounge. Meaning let's go somewhere private and get real biological.

Martha smiled, thinking she'd just heard him say he was willing to give up Sharon Morrisson for her. Now she had something she could hold him to, something she could repeat back to him if necessary. "You said there was nobody special," she could sob. It was like having a strategic nuclear weapon at her disposal. The problem was that they were using the same words but speaking different languages.

After another hour and a few more drinks, Martha finally invited Chuck back to her place, with the idea in her mind that he was hers. And Chuck accepted, with the idea in his mind that he was his own man and none of this had anything to do with anything else. It wasn't until he stepped out of the bar into the wind and starry darkness of the potholed parking lot that he thought maybe a little more explaining was in order. But just as he was thinking this, Martha turned and kissed him, and the thought went clean out of his mind.

A few minutes after this took place, Sharon was driving back from the Mini Mart with some groceries and thought she saw Chuck's car turning off Main Street way up ahead of her. She couldn't imagine why he'd be going in that direction, but when she got home she called his house to see if he was back and, if he was, to ask how things had gone in Amarillo. But there was no answer. Later, after trying his number a couple more times, she fried a pork chop and sat down with it and some potato salad and a beer and had supper.

On the wall next to her refrigerator, beside the *Western Horseman* calendar, Sharon had a little framed drawing of a running horse that an old boyfriend had given her. It always made her think of Chuck, and tonight, as she sat at her solitary meal, she thought about how he seemed to be pulling back from her the last few weeks. She looked at the horse in the picture, and it seemed to be not just running now but running *away*, as if the plastic frame was a corral it wanted out of. When she finished eating and had washed the dishes, she went to bed with a strange, hollow feeling like an unslaked thirst.

That night only one of the three people involved in this story slept well. That was Martha. She'd been lonely ever since she'd ditched Tom Simon, and now she was lying beside a man—a good man (since he'd already received the stamp of approval from Sharon Morrisson) who had (she thought) said he was willing to give up important things for her (which was a prime prerequisite for men in Martha's book).

Chuck, on the other hand, didn't sleep well at all. He felt alternately guilty for lying there next to someone besides Sharon and angry with himself for feeling guilty when what he was doing had nothing to do with Sharon. These two feelings squeezed him like the opposing jaws of a pair of pliers.

Across town Sharon didn't sleep well either. Her dreams were full of galloping horses.

The next morning when Sharon was shuffling around the kitchen in a big T-shirt, making coffee and trying to wake up, Chuck was still at Martha's house wondering if he could slip out of her bed without waking her up. But as he was lying there trying to decide, she did wake up, smiling and beautiful and still enveloped in newness and mystery, and he forgot all about escape.

There were three ways of looking at this situation, one for each person involved. The first way was to view all three parties as free and independent agents. In this interpretation no harm had been done to anybody. The worst that could be said was that Chuck had told Sharon he was going to Amarillo when instead he was going for a drink—a simple lie not much worse than saying you're going to be somewhere at eight o'clock when you know damn well you won't be there till nine. Sharon hadn't been hurt by it. She'd gone grocery shopping, eaten dinner, watched TV, and gone to bed, just as if Chuck had had the drink with some rodeo man. He still felt the same way about her, and he hadn't picked up any diseases. And Martha was better off than before, in the sense that she had spent one night with a man she liked instead of spending it feeling sorry for herself. So the net effect of the whole thing was no worse than even. That was one way of looking at it, the way Chuck would have chosen if he'd had to account for himself.

Another way of looking at it was to see Chuck as having betrayed Sharon: he'd lied to her and cheated on her, given in to his "baser instincts" by going to bed with a woman he hardly even knew. That would have been Sharon's way, if she'd known what was going on.

The third way was that Chuck had found somebody better, and this made all previous contracts open to on-the-spot renegotiation. This would have been Martha's way of seeing things.

These different ways of seeing things didn't come about just because of each person's position in the triangle. And they didn't differ only in who they favored. There was a deeper difference, and a deeper reason for it. In the first view, Chuck's view, all context was pared away. It was like a chess problem or a mathematical formula, generalized and abstract. But in the other two views, Sharon's and Martha's, there was more context than content. The importance of the specific outweighed all general principles, and in the end what mattered was who did what to who and how come. The difference was the difference between the two halves of the human race and how they look at things, the two essential forces balanced against each other—Man and Woman. And the thing that's supposed to keep the forces balanced isn't just power—in this case all three people had plenty of power, more power than they knew what to do with—it's trust. Sometimes it works, and sometimes it doesn't. But nobody ever knows for sure till it's too late.

In a place like Tyrone it's impossible to keep a secret for long. In such a small community the margins between people's lives get blurred, just like in families, and with the same sort of consequences, good and bad. It wasn't long before the local version of the jungle telegraph was carrying the news that Chuck Bonner—you know Chuck, Chuck of Sharon and Chuck? yeah, him—was being seen around with Martha Godley, that new woman in the western-wear shop. In fact, their cars had been seen side by side in the parking lot of the It'll Do Lounge over on the edge of Neptune, which was as good as an admission of hanky-panky. Word was out. Pretty soon everybody knew except Sharon. And eventually she found out too, from her brother Morris's wife, Dawn, who gave her the news with a certain amount of eye-rolling and lip-biting, and with a great deal of sympathy. Weren't men terrible?

It happened one Sunday after dinner when Sharon was at Morris and Dawn's house. Charley was there too. Sharon and Dawn were washing the dishes, and the two brothers were watching a Dallas Cowboys football game on TV in the next room. Their cheering and outbursts of "Get him! Tackle the son of a bitch!" punctuated the revelation in the kitchen, intruding into what Dawn was saying like the chorus in a Greek tragedy. When she finally hit the punch line—"He's been going around with Martha Godley, down at the western store. They've been seen at that little honky-tonk in Neptune"—Sharon's hands stopped moving in the soapy water, and for a minute there was nothing but the sound of a TV commercial in the house. Then the game started again, and she finished the last of the pans and dried her hands and opened a beer and went in and watched the second half with her brothers as if she'd never heard a word.

Of course, her brain was going full speed while she sat there staring at the TV. She couldn't have told you what the score was or who had the ball or anything else. She was in a state of shock, shock deepened by the realization that she should have known. The previous night she'd been at Chuck's house. He'd been very affectionate; if anything, he'd been more affectionate than a few weeks earlier. That in itself should have been suspicious. Also he'd been making a lot of unexplained trips here and there lately, and there'd been nights he hadn't called her and hadn't answered his phone when she called. And now that she thought of it, Martha Godley had had a smug, know-it-all look on her face the last time Sharon had gone in the western-wear shop. Now the blinders were off and the cat was out of the bag. Sharon sat there staring at the football game, trying to decide what she should do.

It was a complicated question, partly because it was embedded in its context like a splinter in the palm of a hand. If she'd wanted, her brothers could have simplified it for her, put it clearly and succinctly and with all the underbrush cleared away: "That son of a bitch's been two-timin' you, Sharon. Ditch him. If you want us to, we'll go give him a thrashing that'll have him limpin' on *both* legs," they might've said. But they were biased and bound to side with their sister, even though they could have found themselves in Chuck's place easy enough. And Sharon had no more interest in stripping away the context than she'd have had in removing a splinter by cutting away the hand around it. The context was the important part as far as she was concerned. She wasn't looking for a general rule here. She was looking for a way to save the best part of the last four years of her life, the man she loved, and her dreams as they'd stretched out in front of her like the unread pages of a book. She wasn't desperate, though (she told herself emphatically), she was pretty enough, and she had men asking her out all the time. If she wanted to, she could tell Chuck to go jump in a lake, and start over with somebody else, no problem. But even if she did that tomorrow—an impossibility, since she knew she'd have to spend a certain amount of time feeling miserable and grieving—she was thirty-two now; she'd be at least thirty-six by the time she'd built up a four-year history with somebody new. Four years of riding horses together and dancing together and laughing together—and even then (as she would have proved by the very process she was considering) it could all be over overnight.

Instead of just quitting, maybe she should go see Chuck and confront him with what she knew. Make him crawl on his belly like a reptile and beg for her forgiveness. That idea had a certain charm, but the longer she thought about it, the less appealing Chuck was in this reptile incarnation. Plus, since he'd already had several weeks' practice lying to her, maybe he'd just deny the whole thing. "Your sister-in-law hasn't got the sense God gave Shetland ponies," she could imagine him saying, and although she knew Dawn was right about this, she also knew Dawn had been wrong about lots of things in the past. So it was plausible, and plausibility is all any good liar needs. If he denied it and explained it away, where would that leave her? She'd either have to believe him or leave him. And she didn't want to do either.

The Cowboys scored against the godless New York Giants and Sharon had to break away from her thoughts to participate in the cheering. Then the extra point went wide of the posts and she sank back into the tangle of her possibilities.

In looking over what she knew and what she wished she knew, Sharon finally realized that the most important question, and the really scary one, was whether or not Chuck still loved her. Everything depended on that. If he did, then these hard questions were worth considering. If he didn't, then she was wasting her time. She might as well watch the last of the game (score: 13 to 14, Giants leading) and then get down to the grieving, the wailing and gnashing of teeth, start counting off the hours of lonely misery until she'd paid her debt of sorrow. So did Chuck love her? She thought back to last night and called up his image on the screen of her imagination and tried to read the look in his eyes. But she discovered she couldn't do it. For the first time, it dawned on her that there were parts of him she could never see into, and parts of her he could never know, things beyond understanding for both of them. It was as if they were of different species. The essential loneliness of the situation, the essential loneliness of life, chilled her like a cold wind on a hard sweat. She got up and went to the bathroom and washed her face and stared at its features in the mirror for a minute. Then she came back out and finished her beer and another and watched the rest of the football game—final score: Cowboys, 20; Giants, 14.

Sharon had planned to spend that evening doing her laundry. Chuck was supposed to be down in Odessa, talking to some people about horses. He'd said he wouldn't be back till late. But she was pretty sure now that he was no nearer Odessa than she was. In fact, she had his location narrowed down to one of two possibilities: either he was at Martha Godley's house, or he was at the It'll Do Lounge planning to go to Martha Godley's house later. She still had a key to his house, so she was pretty sure that he wasn't having Martha into his own bed.

Having narrowed down his probable location, she faced the question of what to do about it. She could track his unseen movements in her head, turning her brain into something like those magnetic transmitters people in James Bond movies were always attaching to each other's cars. But what was the point in that? It would only make her miserable. Sooner or later there would have to be a showdown. So should she wait and catch him *in flagrante delicto*, as the lawyers say, at Martha's house? That would serve him right. But the result, that was the thing: what would be the result?

If she wanted to, she could leave Chuck out of it entirely and make her stand in the western-wear shop. She'd bought enough stuff there over the years and knew Mr. Wild well enough that she might be able to get Martha fired. Even if she couldn't, she was pretty certain she could hit her hard enough to knock her into next week and temporarily mess up her movie-star face. But leaving Chuck out of it didn't seem right. After all, he was the whole point.

She thought all this over, sitting at her dresser, taking down her hair and brushing it out. Then she braided it again and put it back up and started looking through her closet, taking clothes out and throwing them on the bed for consideration as battle dress, then throwing other clothes on top of them, unable to decide, until most of what she owned was piled up on the bedspread and the empty hangers in the closet chimed at her like wind-bells.

About nine o'clock she looked at herself in the full-length mirror. She was dressed as she'd been all day, in a plaid shirt and faded jeans, looking like she always looked except for the extra wear in her face from an afternoon of worry. But how she was dressed didn't matter. She knew that. It was time to get this over with.

The It'll Do sat dark and square in the middle of its dirt parking lot like a bunker for the defense of errors in judgment against the onslaughts of good behavior and clear thinking. Its painted sign stuck up on the roof, illuminated by the beam of a single spotlight in which a hundred moths drew bright erratic circles against the night. Sharon saw Chuck's station wagon and pulled off the road and parked beside it, switching off her car's engine and listening to the silence for a minute before she got out.

It was Sunday night. Earlier Reiley Woodlock had been watching *Bonanza* and more or less ignoring his customers. But it had been over for an hour; Pa and Hoss and Little Joe had vanquished the forces of evil for another week, and all was at peace on the Ponderosa. Now the jukebox was plugged back in and was yelping its songs of lost love out into the darkness of the room. Sharon opened the door beside the old TV and stepped into the bar. Mr. Woodlock saw her and knew she hadn't come to drink. She lacked that hint of furtiveness that people who drank at the It'll Do always had. Maybe her car had broken down and she'd come in to use the phone? No, that wasn't it either. He put his hands on his hips and watched her cross the room.

Martha and Chuck were sitting in the back booth. Because he'd been raised on western stories and knew about the murder of Wild Bill Hickok, Chuck always made it a habit to sit facing the door, and tonight was no exception. But he and Martha were leaning toward each other in the dim, and it wasn't till Sharon had covered half the distance to them that he saw her coming. When he did, his face went burning hot and his fingers went freezing cold. At the same instant, she saw him and hesitated in her stride but then continued. Martha was the last to realize something was up. She didn't know they had company till Sharon's shadow cast itself across Chuck's face.

"Chuck," Sharon said.

And suddenly all the cards were on the table, and all the chips too. There was nothing to deny, no plausible excuse to be made. This was it. They looked at each other across a separation that would have appeared to an outsider to be no more than six feet of smoky air in a dark little bar but that was actually the gulf between men and women, the space between two different and irreconcilable ways of feeling, a gap as wide as the world and as deep as life that couldn't be bridged by knowledge or reason or experimentation—in short a six-foot section of reality.

Sharon started to say more. Her lips moved, but nothing came.

Chuck thought before he acted. What exactly did he want? If he went with Sharon now, would she haul this affair out of the closet some dark night and beat him to death with it? As he looked at her there in that dim light he realized there was no way of knowing. He either had to trust her or forget her.

He looked at Martha again. Tears were sparkling on her long eyelashes—tears of anger, shame, sorrow, love, who knows? Real tears anyway. For a moment they were frozen there, like a diorama in the Museum of Human Relations. Then he stood up.

Sharon didn't push for more. Her question had been answered as far as it could be. The song on the jukebox ended and was replaced by another just as sad. Chuck stood there, wondering why he didn't feel embarrassed, then he said good night to Martha and walked over to the bar and settled up with Mr. Woodlock, giving him some extra in case she wanted another drink after he was gone. And then he and Sharon walked out through the wailing music, past the flickering TV, into the dark, and he drove away in his car and she drove away in hers.

9

Chuck Bonner

The biggest thrill Chuck had ever known was sitting on a bad horse waiting for the lunge into the ring, the lunge that made his teeth rattle and his heart jump right out of his chest. It was a thrill he'd discovered early, and by the time he graduated from high school he'd decided to follow it, although years later, looking back, he couldn't recall exactly when the idea of being a rodeo rider had come to him. It seemed to have just always been a part of him. He was good at it, though, and made enough money to keep body and soul together, and that was all he needed. When anybody asked him why he traveled around risking his neck on bad horses for very little pay, he'd just say, "They pay me. It's a job." It seemed too personal to try to explain why he really did it.

He rode broncs until the end of his thirtieth year. That year he was on a hot streak, drawing good buckers and riding them all, enjoying it, and enjoying the money too. For the first time ever, when he went into a restaurant he could leave a good tip, and people treated him like a professional instead of like a rodeo bum. He thought it would go on and on. But then, on the final day of the Tom Green County Roundup down in San Angelo, he drew a big albino stallion named White Lightning and everything changed.

The horse didn't look like anything special. It was tall and pink-eyed and had big, flat hooves that turned out like the toes of a ballet dancer, but as far as Chuck could tell it was still just livestock. Only this time, when he got on and his name was called and the gate opened, something went wrong. Instead of bucking out into the arena, this horse just stayed right where it was, in that little chute, and began bucking against the tall wooden sides, not going into the ring at all. Chuck was like a man trapped in a phone booth with a thunderstorm. His boot caught on a rail and he felt his ankle snap, and then he began to slide out of the saddle. Next thing he knew he was on the ground under those big hooves. The last image his mind registered before he woke up in the hospital was of that horse looking down at him the way a housewife might look at a cockroach.

He stayed in the hospital for two weeks while the doctors tried to put him back together, and when he finally went home encased in plaster, his rodeo days were over. Six months later he was walking pretty good again, but already he'd begun to speak in the third person of the days when he'd ridden broncs, as if that former self were just some guy he'd once met in a bar, no one he really had anything to do with.

On a crisp, cloudless morning in the autumn of his thirty-fifth year, Chuck Bonner hitched a horse trailer to the back of his station wagon and headed off down the road that led away from his house and barn. The sun shone straight into his eyes, and the narrow two-lane reflected it like a strip of sheet metal. A hundred miles east, down in the rough country off the edge of the caprock, was the little town of Fenceline, where Chuck was supposed to meet an old man named Hub Marsdon to see about buying some buckers. The two of them had met at auctions several times in the past few years. Both of them had ridden the rodeo, although Marsdon had stopped long before Chuck had started, and now they were both horse traders, rodeo contractors. Only Marsdon was ready to retire, getting out of the bucking-horse business. That was why Chuck was going to see him. He'd been offered first pick of the stock. Hoping to find some good bargains, he'd filled his pockets with all the cash he could lay his hands on, and the unaccustomed feel of money in his jeans made him whistle as he drove along.

When he got to Fenceline, he stopped at the one and only gas station in town and asked directions. Hub's place was at the end of a long, crooked dirt road that ran out of town into the surrounding mesquite thickets. It was a fairly extensive horse operation, sprawling and tumbledown. There were six big barns and three little ones, plenty of corrals, lots of trailers parked here and there, and four old pickups in various states of decay lined up along the back fence like an exhibit on automotive decomposition. The old man had just finished feeding his horses and was drinking coffee when Chuck arrived.

"How you doin', Chuck? Find me okay?"

"Mornin', Hub. How you doin'?"

They spent several hours wandering from barn to barn, looking at horses and talking about the weather, the rodeo season, this and that. Then finally in early afternoon, when they'd seen everything there was to see and it had gotten pretty hot, they went back to Hub's office, an old ten-foot travel trailer that sat permanently chocked up on concrete blocks at one end of the long alley between the two biggest barns. No doubt it had begun life a bright canary-yellow, but over the years the sun had faded it until now it was the color of old dentures. The word OFFICE was hand-lettered over the door in flaking paint. Inside, the walls were decorated with framed eight-by-tens. Layers and layers of snapshots had been stuck in the frames around them until it wasn't easy to tell what the original photographs were of. There were also a molting deer's head and two feed-company calendars. Hub made his way through tilting pagodas of old magazines to a desk.

"Take a seat. I think I got some beers here," he said. He dug into a little, half-size refrigerator, handed a bottle to Chuck, and motioned him toward a folding chair. Then they began to do their business.

Until now they had just looked at animals and talked about them in general terms. But now they sipped their beers and smiled at each other and started maneuvering toward the deals they had in mind. Figures were occasionally mentioned and were batted around for a while until they became specific or dropped out of sight; offers were proposed and discarded and reproposed in different words. Mostly the two men told rodeo stories, and it took a long time. They finished their beers, drank another pair, and then another after that. The stories got better and better.

"I tell you, old Bubba coulda rode a bolt o' lightnin' that day...."

"... stood up on its hind legs like a man and started marchin' across the arena...."

"... I thought these two cowgirls were gonna kill me if I didn't get out...."

"... fine a bucker as you'll find in Texas...."

"... took the rifle out o' his back window and aimed it at this fella's hat...."

"... had a horse sort of like that buckskin of yours, only it was a real bad bucker. One of those *real* serious bucking horses...."

And on and on and on.

Somewhere in the middle of the fourth or fifth beer, after they'd made a deal for three horses, Chuck happened to look out through the screen door and see a big white horse walking toward him from the far end of the alley between the barns. Riding it was a little girl, her face dark in the shade of her hat brim. His beer stopped partway to his open mouth, and he froze in that pose like a person caught in an unexpected snapshot.

Hub didn't notice because by now he was in full voice. He had just been explaining how a longhorn bull bucks differently from a Brahma, and speculating that he might be the last man alive to have been fool enough to ride a longhorn, and, seeing no interruptions, he was segueing into a story about how he'd once ridden a bull buffalo in a rodeo up in Canada when he was a young man, fifty years ago. He was saying, ". . . so I said I would, like the blame' fool I was in those days, and went out and climbed over the chute. Well, just as I was settlin' on his back I noticed up among the cowboys sittin' there watchin' me was a preacher we called Burn-'em Bailey and another fellow I knew I'd seen but didn' reco'nize at the moment. Anyway, this big ol' buffalo he was . . . he was . . ." And it was at this point he finally noticed that Chuck was staring out the door. He leaned over to see what the attraction was.

"Mandy," he yelled when he saw the little girl, "you walk him on 'round there to Pedro, honey, and he'll unsaddle him for you. And make sure you don't step in none of that manure this time. Your mama'll skin me alive if you ruin those new boots."

"Okay, Paw-Paw," the little girl said in a high voice like a birdcall.

He turned back to Chuck. "That's my great-granddaughter."

Chuck's beer finally made it to his mouth and he drained it. Then he said, "How long you had that horse?"

"Oh, couple o' years I guess," Hub said. "Never owned a albino before. Peculiar animal. Used to be a bad bucker. Real mean bastard, from what I heard. S'posed to've even killed somebody. Old Dickerson down in McKenzie had him—you know old man Dickerson, don't you?—and I picked him up as a gimme in a trade for some mixed bulls, thinkin' he'd be an attraction, bein' a albino and all. Turns out he's gentle as a lamb. Bucked hisself out, I guess. Calm as anything now."

The girl dismounted at a tall wooden step beside one of the barns. The horse stood still while she did, and it seemed to Chuck to be looking at him.

"What's his name?" Chuck asked. The animal's ears shifted back and forth under a sparkling halo of flies.

"Mandy. She's my oldest granddaughter's baby. Real sweet little girl. Smart as a whip too. Be a barrel racer someday, I bet. Her mama used to be a fine one 'fore she got married."

"I mean the horse. What's he called?"

"Oh . . . he was called Lightnin' or Thunder or somethin' like that. Some kinda' weather, I b'lieve. But we call him Silver after the Lone Ranger's horse. You know, 'Hi-yo Silver, awayyyy.' Don't make no difference what you call a horse anyway. I cain't sell him, though, if that's what you're workin' up to, Chuck. I'd like to oblige you, but it'd be like sellin' her puppy dog. 'Sides, he's not much of a animal anymore. Too old. Gelded besides. Now if you want a ridin' horse, I just happen to have some real good ones at the moment. I can make you a hot deal on a little roan mare I been trainin' for the last couple o' months. Sweetest-handlin' animal you ever saw; got a mouth like velvet. Turn on a dime and give you nine cents change. Make a hell of a cuttin' pony with somebody like you in the saddle."

The little girl led the horse to the far end of the barn and turned out of sight.

"I don't want him," Chuck said with a mechanical little laugh. "He just looked kind of . . . familiar for a minute. I already got all the horses I can stand and you've about cleaned me out for cash. So . . . you were telling me about a buffalo. . . ."

"Oh, yeah," the old man said, forgetting instantly about the horse and picking up the thread of his interrupted story. "So, there was old Burn-'em and this other fella sittin' there behind the chute like a pair of buzzards on a dead branch. Just then the boys opened the gate, and that buffalo shot out o' there frog-walkin' like you never seen and bellerin' like a banshee! I looked over and saw that preacher smilin' like a dog, and then's when it came to me who the other guy was and I knew I'd made a serious mistake. . . ."

He kept talking and talking. Chuck listened, nodding politely, but his mind was somewhere else, fallen away from the here and now entirely.

Late in the afternoon, after drinking a few more beers and getting rid of more of his money than he'd intended, Chuck loaded four newly acquired horses into his trailer and took off for home. Hub stood by the main barn and waved him down the dirt road till they were cut off from each other by the cloud of dust.

There was no question that the albino horse was the same one that had nearly killed him. He ought to know. He'd seen it often enough in his dreams: big as a locomotive, white as skim milk, with eyes the color of rubies and hooves the size of overturned washtubs. Of course, in real life it hadn't been anything like that. Just a big white horse with splayed-out hooves and pink albino eyes—a nag for little girls to ride. A chill went through Chuck like a gust of wind through a pasture, and an image of his younger self suddenly came back to him like the face of a forgotten lover. He shook his head and rubbed his eyes. In a field to his left, in the horizontal light of the waning day, a green John Deere tractor moved along like a giant beetle, its windows opaque yellow in the glare of the declining sun.

When he got to the edge of Tyrone, he pulled into the parking lot of the liquor store and went in.

"Hi, Leon."

Leon was leaning over the counter, staring silently out the front window, mesmerized by the spinning blades of a windmill across the road. "Chuck," he said, still staring.

Chuck looked around at the shelves of bottles, wondering what to get. He didn't drink often, but since he already had an edge on from drinking beer all afternoon with Hub, it seemed like he should keep going. Finish the job.

He picked up a pint bottle from a whiskey display and hefted it in his hand, trying to decide how drunk it would make him and if that was what he wanted.

"It's on special," Leon said.

Chuck looked around at him.

His eyes were still fixed on the windmill, and he looked as if he hadn't blinked in about an hour. "A buck off on the fifths. Sixty cents on the pints." His voice was like the voice of a hypnotist's volunteer.

Chuck carried the bottle to the register and paid for it. In the parking lot he unscrewed the cap and took a long, burning swallow, watching out of the corner of his eye as the low sun silhouetted a caricature of him on the side of the horse trailer. Then he got in his car and drove back onto the road.

When he got home, he unloaded the new horses. Each was put into a stall in the big barn and given plenty of fresh water and a bucketful of oats. When the last one had been made at home, Chuck stood in the open space between the stalls and took the bottle out of his pocket again and drank. The barn had four skylights in the roof. He looked at them as he tilted his head back. Each showed an identical patch of darkening blue. It was like the hold of a ship. In the daytime there were columns of sunshine that came down from them, sparkling with dust motes and flakes of hay that made the barn like the inside of a cathedral, and the smell of feed and horseshit was as rich as incense. But tonight it was a freighter floating away in the dusk.

The whiskey was more than half empty now and sloshed when he put it back in his pocket. He could feel the missing ounces pumping through his veins like some sort of lubricant.

Outside the sun had disappeared and left the sky as garish as a cheap calendar. When he walked to the house, the ground seemed unsteady and slightly springy under his feet and reminded him of walking on his parents' bed when he was very small. The porch pitched a little as he stepped onto it. He held on to a pillar and waited for it to settle, then he went to the door and fumbled with his key at the lock. As if triggered by this, the telephone began to ring. At first its steady bleat made him hurry to open the door, but then he stopped and leaned his head against the frame and listened, sensing claustrophobia and depression waiting inside like muggers. He left the keys in the lock and eased the screen door quietly to and went to the corner of the porch and leaned against the pillar there, looking out across the yard.

Birds the color of shadows were sweeping the thickening air around the barn. The phone stopped ringing. He took the bottle out again and brought it up to his eye, holding it so that he could look across the liquid's shiny surface. A lake of cheap whiskey. He tilted the bottle to his lips and felt the liquid gush into his mouth. The light and the whiskey were reflections of each other, both melting away until the bottle contained nothing but night. The birds dissolved in the dark, leaving only their high-pitched squeaks behind, trailing in the air like invisible streamers.

When it was completely dark, Chuck stooped and carefully set the empty bottle down. Then he stepped off the porch into the soft starlight of the yard and crossed the open space and slipped into the barn's shadow like a man sinking into a bath of ink.

Opening the door, he could hear the horses breathing all around him. One snorted. Another stamped its hoof. They could see him against the square of night he stood in, but he could only hear and smell them.

In the first stall was a young stallion, one of the animals he'd bought from Hub. He thought of how it looked, the flare of its nostrils, and went toward it with his hands held out until he felt the rough boards of the stall, then he groped along them to the corner and found a halter and four feet of lead rope hanging there on a nail. He took it down and shook the tangles out.

The stallion whinnied nervously and backed into the corner of the stall as the gate creaked.

" 'Sokay. 'Sokay. Mmmmm-hmmmmm," Chuck said quietly.

After a moment his hands found the animal's neck and felt the muscles twitch along it. The horse's ears lay flat as Chuck slipped the halter on.

He led the horse out of the barn and watched it take shape in the dim light—a moving black cutout swinging tensely at the end of its tether. Once he had it in the middle of the open space, he worked his way around beside it.

"Whoa, boy. Whoooa," he said under his breath.

The horse kept shifting away. Then for a moment it held.

"Jus' let me get up and we'll . . . whoa . . . whoa now." And he swung up onto the stallion's back. It was bucking and twisting before his leg even crossed it.

A moment later he was sitting on the ground, listening to the roar in his ears. Off to his left the stallion slowed to a trot and then stopped and looked back at him warily. Chuck rubbed his bad leg and sighed and lay back in the dirt, feeling all his bones shift inside him.

There was no moon and the sky was dark as only a country sky can be; the stars were like bright pellet holes in a high tin roof where someone had blasted it with a shotgun. It made him think of another night years before when he'd come through town on his way from one rodeo to another. He'd felt lonely, so he'd gone out to Bigger 'n Dallas hoping to run into some friendly woman, but instead he'd ended up drinking alone. Just before closing time two fellows had started a fight on the dance floor and carried it out into the parking lot. Chuck helped break it up. After the combatants had been put in their cars and sent home, he found himself standing there in the dark with the old man who owned the bar. It was summer and very warm, and neither of them was in a hurry to go back inside, so they talked for a few minutes. Somehow the subject of stars came up, and the old man began pointing out constellations, calling their names like they were local citizens—Hercules, Orion, Andromeda, Perseus, Pegasus. . . . Pegasus, Chuck recalled, was a horse with wings. He blinked at the pattern above him and wondered where Pegasus was tonight. And what it would be like to ride a horse made of stars.

10

Diane Ghertz Wintergarten

In high school, twenty years ago, Diane had been a twirler with the marching band. Not just *a* twirler but the *head* twirler, with a red-sequined costume that fit like a reptile's skin, white vinyl boots with tassels at the back, a rhinestone tiara, and a tiny gold bracelet with a little heart on it that Jerry Wintergarten had given her for Valentine's Day. Her hair was done up stiff and gleaming in a tall, gauzy beehive that sparkled with hair spray in the lights of the playing field. There had been three twirlers: Diane and Marsha Wilbur and Nan Jennings. But Diane was in charge. She thought up all the twirling routines, and she was the best twirler, the star.

For the first half of every football game the cheerleaders were the center of attention, jumping around and yelling themselves hoarse—"Siss-Boom-Bahh! Siss-Boom-Bahh! Push 'em back! Push 'em back, waaaaayyyy back"—but at halftime, when the players limped off to the dressing room and the band marched out onto the field, then the twirlers took over, shucking their long coats and prancing out along the fifty-yard line like nervous racehorses. And they made the cheerleaders look like nothing. The twirlers didn't jump around and yell. They didn't have to. They were *artistes*, girls who could dance with the primal forces of nature. The band played, the lights reflected on their sequined uniforms, and they made their batons spin so that they changed from sticks into wheels of transparent metal. Diane could spin faster than anybody—and her baton took on a life of its own, leaping out of her hand and going high up in the air to hover for an instant above her like a halo. When it came down, she'd catch it perfectly, gracefully, like it was nothing at all, like she could do it in her sleep. After the band played the school song and marched off the field with her and Marsha and Nan leading them, she'd look around at the cheerleaders again. They always looked sullen. They knew they'd been topped.

In her senior year Diane twirled torches. Mr. Morton, the band director, tried to talk her out of it. "It's too dangerous, Diane," he said. But she knew she could do it; she could feel the power in her hands. So in early November, in the big game against Neptune, partway through the halftime show the main lights were switched off, leaving only the safety lights burning (Diane had wanted total darkness, but Mr. Morton pointed out that the band wouldn't be able to read the music), and Diane slipped her dad's Zippo out of the leg of her costume and lit her torch batons—whoosh, whoosh. Then the band started playing the theme from *El Cid*, and she threw the flaming batons higher and higher, spinning them like circles of lightning. In the stunned silence of the crowd, in the spaces between the notes of the slow, majestic music, over the gasps of her own breath, she could hear the whisper of the spinning flames as they went up into the night sky and came down again and again. On either side of her, like a magician's assistants, Nan and Marsha stood, toes pointed, smiles brightly fixed, their eyes reflecting the burning batons. After her last perfect toss, the lights came back up, the band played something fast, the flames were extinguished, and the game went on, an anticlimax now.

She did this every Friday night until school let out for

Christmas. Seven games. Seven performances with the torch batons. Between the games she and Marsha and Nan practiced their routines on Wednesday nights and Fridays at noon. Diane used her regular batons for these rehearsals. The only time she practiced with torches was when she was alone. About once a week she'd borrow her daddy's car on some pretext or other and drive out into the country on an old road nobody used anymore. When she was away from town, she'd park on a quiet turn-row, switch off the headlights, and light up her batons. Then she'd do her routines to the music in her head, with only the stars for an audience. That was when she threw highest and spun fastest and came closest to perfection. The only times anybody saw her do this were once when old man Kirby went out looking for his dog that had run off and spotted the batons going up and down and reported it as a UFO to the sheriff's office, and once when Jerry talked her into it when they'd gone out parking. After she'd done it for him, he'd kissed her and kissed her and tried to get his hands under her clothes. He'd been crazy for her that night.

Diane's last performance took place at the football game against O'Donnell just before Christmas. The night was bitter-cold, and a fierce north wind blew passes out of the hands of receivers all during the first half. By morning everything would be covered with snow and there'd be drifts three feet high across the roads. Marsha, who hadn't been twirling for but five years, was afraid she wouldn't be able to handle the wind, but Nan and Diane told her there was only one way to learn, and that was to just do it. The band marched out onto the field like a little army marching into a winter campaign. The metal of the batons felt like clear ice and the wind pulled at the girls' rigid hairdos as if it wanted to blow them along like tumbleweeds. After the halftime preliminaries were out of the way—a couple of marches and a Broadway-show tune—the lights dimmed, and Diane saw Mr. Morton look around at her, looking to see if she was really going to throw torches in this wind. She smiled at him and slipped the Zippo out with stiff fingers and lit up. The music started.

The flames of the twirling batons seemed different in the extreme cold, almost fragile. The wind blew them into tatters against the darkness. In the gusts the batons wouldn't throw straight and seemed to arc away from her and fall back unpredictably as if they were trying to escape into the sky. But Diane hadn't dropped a baton in a performance since she was twelve years old, and she didn't intend to now. She concentrated on the spinning shafts until everything else just disappeared—the cold biting through her costume, the tears the wind brought to her eyes, the rough spot in the ground where a cleated boot had torn up the grass. The batons went up and down, up and down.

As the theme from *El Cid* came to its finale, it looked as if things were going to be okay, as if Diane would accomplish the impossible again. But then, on the last big chord, when she was supposed to do her highest throw and spin around twice and catch the batons above her head in a cross, the wind suddenly gusted as if it wanted to blow out the flames entirely. She threw, spun, reached up, and found one of the batons four inches farther away than she'd expected. In an instant that seemed to stretch like the slow-motion replay in a TV football game she had to choose between letting it fall or catching it too near the end, and Diane, who'd never dropped a baton, felt her freezing fingers close on the hot metal, felt the fluttering flame lick her wrist, and the soft skin burn as the baton stopped, secure, undropped, so close to perfect nobody but she could know there'd been a problem.

After they marched off the field, she had to go get something put on the burn, and it took weeks for the blisters to go away. She carried them like stigmata right through

Christmas and New Year's, her injured hand wrapped in soft white gauze, and was almost disappointed when the burn left no scar at all.

Sometime in the ensuing twenty years, during which she married Jerry, gave birth to their daughter, Lucille, and came into possession of all the things she ever thought she wanted—a Cadillac Coupe de Ville with power windows, a big brick house with refrigerated air-conditioning, a dishwasher, a washer and dryer, and a maid who came twice a week—sometime in those two decades Diane came to feel as if one way or another she'd dropped the baton of her life, made some choice without knowing it, or taken a wrong turn at some obscure crossroads she hadn't even seen. Either that or she'd peaked too soon, hitting her high point at seventeen years old and leaving nothing for the rest of her life but the long slide to old age. This feeling came to her more and more as time went on. Sometimes she'd wake up in the morning with it, like a hangover, and it would dog her steps all day.

If it had been anything less than the questioning of her entire existence, she could have talked about it with her friend Bobbi Jo Tarbuckle in one of their never-ending phone conversations. But what would Bobbi Jo have thought if she'd called up and said, "Hey, you know what, Bobbi Jo? I think I screwed up sometime after high school, and I may have ruined my whole life." I mean, what could a person say to that? "Don't worry about it"? "It'll be okay"? Bobbi Jo thought life was roses and sunshine, or ought to be. She had a pair of the cutest little five-year-old twin girls named Bobbi and Jo, and she didn't want to hear about how somebody thought she had taken a wrong turn twenty years ago and screwed up her whole life, even if that somebody was her best friend in the whole world. Hell, Bobbi Jo didn't even want to hear about the trouble Lucille was getting into. In fact, the *last* thing she wanted to hear about was how her beautiful twin girls might turn into little sluts in another ten years or so. What Bobbi Jo wanted to hear about was good babysitters who worked cheap, and easy diet plans that allowed chocolate, and what was on sale in the Hemphill-Wells store up in Lubbock.

So Diane was stuck with this feeling she didn't talk about. And like a dog that's never let out for exercise, the idea kept running back and forth in the confines of her brain, going over and over the same ground. What exactly were the symptoms? she would ask herself, imagining herself as a doctor in a white coat with a stethoscope hanging around her neck like a good-luck charm. Well, there was the fact that she was tired all the time and had gotten to the point of sleeping at least ten hours a day, sometimes twelve. She'd slip off when nobody was looking and take a little snooze, the way a secret tippler might slip off and take a little snort. Nobody between the ages of three and ninety-five should sleep as much as she did. That was one thing. And there was the feeling that she was becoming invisible. She could see herself okay, but sometimes other people had trouble seeing her. Whenever she and Lucille went somewhere together, it seemed as if everybody could see Lucille just fine, but nobody saw her at all anymore, like she was just a shadow, a nothing, like when you're watching TV and the sound keeps going, but instead of the picture there is just a sign saying

> WE ARE CURRENTLY
> EXPERIENCING DIFFICULTIES
> WITH THE VIDEO PORTION
> OF THIS PROGRAM.
> PLEASE STAY TUNED.

Maybe the more she slept, the more invisible she got, like her visibility was leaking out in her dreams, or like that movie she remembered seeing at the drive-in when she was in high school about vampires drinking people's blood at night. Or it could be a symptom of some kind of weird medical thing—Invisible Man Syndrome, something a TV doctor might diagnose. Or maybe—and she thought about this a lot—it happened to everybody, but nobody talked about it, same as they didn't talk about death or sex. Diane tried to picture her mother with video trouble but couldn't. 'Course, if she *had* had video trouble, she'd never have mentioned it to Diane. After the accident with Lucinda's eye, she never trusted Diane with anything, no matter how good she tried to be, and the only thing important she ever told her was on the night before she married Jerry, by which time she'd already known. Diane wished she had somebody to talk to about how she felt, about the invisibility and the tiredness. But she didn't. Not Bobbi Jo and not Lucinda and not Mama and certainly not Lucille.

"Hey, Lucille? Sit down, honey. I want to talk to you about something important," she imagined herself saying. "You know, when you get older, you're suddenly going to want to go into hibernation, and you'll start feeling invisible too. I'll be darned if I know what you're supposed to do about it, but I just thought you'd like to know what's coming so you can get ready whatever way you think best."

They'd lock her in the state mental hospital down in Big Spring if she started talking like that. And Lucille would just laugh at her.

Diane got up from the kitchen table and went to the counter and made herself another cup of instant coffee. Outside the sun was blazing away on the September lawn. She could feel it where it shone through the window onto her hands. She never went out in the sun much anymore. Not since she'd heard on the *Paul Harvey Show* that it could cause premature aging. She'd tried to tell Lucille about that because she was always sunbathing out in the backyard in her bikini, but Lucille just got irritated and pretended she didn't hear, as if Diane were no more than a gnat buzzing around.

She finished her coffee down to the undissolved sludge in the bottom, then put the cup in the dishwasher next to Jerry's breakfast dishes and the dishes from supper the night before and the dishes from various snacks in between, and she looked around for any other dishes she'd missed. There was a knife with butter smeared along the blade. She threw it in. There was another coffee cup. Her cereal bowl. A long wooden mixing spoon.... Diane put them in the dishwasher as she found them. But when she picked up the spoon she stopped and stood in the middle of the kitchen, holding it, looking at it, and suddenly she realized what its shape reminded her of. Her fingers began to move, stiffly at first, like a couple who haven't danced for a long time finding their way into the music, then faster and faster until the spoon was spinning like a propeller, awkwardly, because it wasn't long enough and the balance was bad, but spinning nonetheless. Then she tried a toss and smashed the light fixture on the ceiling and everything fell to the floor—glass, spoon, and all.

For a moment she stood there, looking at the pattern of glass on the linoleum, with an expression on her face like someone who'd been startled awake. Then she stooped over and picked everything up, pitched it in the trash, tossed the spoon into the dishwasher, and went out and got into her Cadillac and left.

The road to Lubbock was perfectly straight after she hit the main highway, and it only took her about an hour to get to where she was going.

The woman who ran the shop was short, with pudgy little hands like a child's that ended in long, dangerous-looking nails. Diane thought with a pang of sympathy that she'd probably once been described as petite. Her small size was accented by a tall, bouffant hairdo that looked both familiar and antique, like something from your grandmother's attic that's been donated to the museum and shows up in an exhibit, and she wore it with defiant pride.

"Help you?" she asked.

"Yes. You got any torch batons?" Diane said.

"You looking for electric or the real thing?"

"Real thing."

"Your daughter have any experience with them? They can be pretty dangerous."

"They're not for my daughter. They're for me. I can handle them. I do triples, back reverses, double turns, take-aways, in-and-outs. And I'd . . . I . . . misplaced my old ones," Diane had started out in a rush, trying to sound like a professional twirler but then realized there was no such thing. "I used to twirl a lot," she concluded, her voice winding down like an old-fashioned alarm clock at the end of its ring.

She and the short woman with the high hairdo looked at each other for a minute. Then without saying anything else, the woman turned and began searching through a stack of boxes behind the counter that looked like what piano rolls come in, except longer. Once she paused and glanced up at Diane, gauging her size as she might gauge the weight of a roast, then she went back to the stack, finally picking out two identical boxes.

"These what you had in mind?" she asked, laying them on the scratched-up glass countertop beneath which lay rhinestone tiaras and pom-poms and tassels and a little hand-lettered sign saying

Give Your Daughter The Confidence
That Only Twirling Can Impart

Diane opened one box and slid out the baton with its tissue-paper wrapping. It had a gold-sparkle shaft. Two inches at each end were covered with fluffy white wicking. It was brilliant even in the dull fluorescent light of the shop, and she could almost hear marching-band music when she touched it, as if the notes were somehow trapped in the sparkles.

"Yes, these'll do fine. They're real nice," she said. "Who do I make the check out to?"

"The Little Princess Shop."

Diane wrote out the check and signed it with a flourish.

When the woman put the batons in a sack, she said, "Won't be as easy as you remember," giving Diane that look again, one veteran to another.

"I've been burned before," Diane said.

The woman snorted and said something under her breath that sounded like "Haven't we all, honey" but might as easily have been "All right, it's your money."

On the drive home Diane kept looking at herself in the rearview mirror.

11

Jerry Wintergarten

Jerry Wintergarten was a man who tried to do right. He believed in taking the main roads, obeying the speed limit, and getting good advice and following it. He liked to keep his life running smooth and level like a well-piloted airplane: insurance always paid up, car always washed, and his business—the Wintergarten Cotton Gin, which he'd taken over from his father—always running in the black. Every morning, Monday through Friday, he got up at six-thirty, ate one egg, two strips of crisp bacon, two pieces of toast, and drank a cup of coffee, and as he ate he listened to the farm report on the Lubbock radio station, paying special attention to the cotton prices and crop forecasts. In the ginning season he was in the office by seven-thirty and might stay there till seven in the evening or even later. During the rest of the year he didn't go in until eight, but he still got up at six-thirty because he wanted to hear the farm report over his breakfast and because he liked to be regular about things.

In the other parts of his life Jerry was also very regular. At twenty years old, he had married his high-school sweetheart, Diane, who was a year younger than he was. They'd married after a short engagement while he was a student at West

Texas State College, studying Agricultural Economics, preparing himself to work at the cotton gin. When they first got married, he and Diane lived in a little garage apartment not far from the campus. She enrolled in the Home Ec department and took a few courses until Jerry was ready to graduate. During that time they occasionally invited other young married couples over for dinner. They would open a bottle of cheap wine and eat spaghetti and laugh about how poor they all were. Sometimes they played records on an old hi-fi and danced around the sparsely furnished living room, bumping into one another between the coffee table and the bookshelf. If it was football season, they went to the home games and cheered for the team. At halftime Diane would take Jerry's binoculars and watch the twirlers perform with the marching bands. She had been a twirler in high school, and she would pass comments on the girls' performances with the air of a professional critic. This always impressed Jerry. He often thought about how she had looked in her twirler's uniform, how it had made her sparkle in the lights. It still hung at one end of the closet in the little garage apartment, and sometimes he wished she would put it on again. He'd always wanted to take it off her. He thought it would be like peeling a big exotic fruit. The idea excited him a great deal. Sometimes when he was sitting in one of his economics classes, he would start to think about this and his mind would drift away from whatever was being said and he'd go into a sort of trance. We're married now, husband and wife, he'd think. Why shouldn't I peel her out of her twirler's uniform like a big exotic fruit? She doesn't use it for anything else. But he was always too embarrassed to mention it to Diane. He was afraid she would think he was strange. Once, after one of their spaghetti dinners when he had drunk a little more wine than usual, he almost asked. Maybe if he'd had one more glass he would have.

After he graduated from college, they moved back to Tyrone and he went to work at the gin. He'd worked there before, in the summers, but only as a sort of office boy–day laborer–general factotum. Now he had a degree in agricultural economics with a minor in accounting, so he wore a tie to work and sat in the office behind a desk most of the time. At first he didn't make much money. His father didn't believe in paying him a lot just because he was family. But after a few years, when he had proven his value to the business, he made plenty. Then when he and Diane had other young married couples over for dinner, they didn't have spaghetti anymore. They had bar-b-q if it was warm enough to cook outside, fried chicken if it wasn't. Jerry cooked the bar-b-q on a big brick grill in the backyard. Diane cooked the chicken at the stove. She had a very good recipe that she'd learned when she was studying Home Ec, and people always complimented her on it. The men told Jerry how lucky he was to be married to Diane because she was such a fine cook and kept the house so nice and still had the good looks of a twirler. Some of the women also told Diane how lucky she was to have Jerry; he worked so hard and provided for her so well and had such a good bar-b-q–sauce recipe. And some of them also said privately, when they were alone with her in the kitchen, that their own husbands were disappointments; they drank too much or ran around on them or were lazy. And over the space of a year, two of the men confided to Jerry while they were alone around the bar-b-q grill that their wives were not what they'd hoped; they were either cold or they nagged or they were letting themselves go all to hell. Jerry felt embarrassed when they told him this. But he also felt lucky and smart, like things were paying off, like there was a certain righteous justice to life.

After he and Diane had been married for three years, they had a daughter. Her name was Lucille. Diane picked out the name. They had an agreement that she could name the girls and Jerry could name the boys. She named the little girl

Lucille because her sister's name was Lucinda. She'd been going to name the baby after her sister, but halfway through writing it on the form her hand had suddenly changed course and written *Lucille* instead. Jerry never got to name a son. He would have named him after himself if he'd had the chance—Jerry Junior—but Lucille was the only child they had.

After Lucille was born, he and Diane only invited couples with young babies over to dinner. Those who didn't have babies seemed inexplicably bored by Lucille and the cute things she did and the cute stories Jerry and Diane told about her. But people with babies were able to tell their own cute baby stories and were much more interesting company.

Jerry's father gave him a big raise after Lucille came, and he moved his family into a nice house on the other side of town from the gin, and he bought a secondhand car for Diane so she could do her errands and see her friends whenever she wanted to.

Ten years later Jerry's father retired from the business and Jerry took it over. It prospered under his care. For thirteen years he'd had his own ideas about how things ought to be done, and now he was able to put them into effect. He expanded, borrowed a little to buy new equipment, hired a couple of new people, and made a lot of money by working hard and smart and not rocking the boat. Life had enough risks without taking unnecessary ones, he figured. The bottom could fall out of the cotton market tomorrow; some scientist somewhere could invent a new synthetic fabric and they'd all go bust; a tornado could destroy the gin and leave him with nothing. It would be tempting fate to take unnecessary risks—buying foreign cars or taking up with strange women or playing poker, for instance. And it wasn't as if he didn't have any fun. He did. But his fun was the kind a mechanic has seeing a motor he's fixed run smoothly, the kind a weatherman has seeing the sunshine he's predicted come to pass. It was a calm satisfaction, a kind of peace. He had his business, his lovely wife, his cute daughter, his good health, and a bank account full of money. He had exactly what he wanted out of life, and he credited it all to following the rules scrupulously. Sometimes he even felt as if he was within spitting distance of some ultimate unseen goal, although he wasn't sure what that might be. In occasional dreamy moments he imagined life as a football game in which his team had carefully and cautiously run up a winning score, and any minute now the referee would blow a whistle and declare them the victors and things would achieve a kind of happy stasis, like a finished painting framed and hanging on a wall. He tried to communicate some of this to the Sunday School class he taught: "A wise man will hear and will increase learning, and a man of understanding shall attain unto wise council . . . but fools despise wisdom and instruction."

But a couple of years later things began to go wrong. Jerry liked to attach specific causes to things, and in this case the first cause of the trouble seemed to be the abduction of his sweet little daughter and her replacement with a surly, unreasonable teenager who bore the same name but had nothing else in common with the little golden-haired child he loved so much. Of course, he knew the pouty pubescent kid who sat across the table at dinner was really just Lucille "going through a phase," as the books said, but sometimes he could hardly believe it. What's happened to her? he'd ask himself when she showed up wearing some outrageous outfit or began talking about things that shouldn't have concerned her at all. She'd been such a sweet little girl. They'd dressed her in frilly petticoats, and he'd carried her everywhere to keep her from getting dirty. And now . . . They'd spoiled her. That was the problem. His wife and his mother had spoiled her rotten. He could see it now, when it was too late. Lucille had no idea how the world worked, what the rules were. That was why she acted the way she did, why she made those crazy, infuriating statements she was always coming out with.

Jerry couldn't figure out how to cope with her. She wouldn't listen to reason at all. Gradually their relationship changed from that of proud father and beloved daughter to that of two implacable opponents dealing with each other through strategy and power. He might not be able to persuade her not to do certain things, but he could thwart her sometimes. Although even that became difficult after her grandmother, his own mother, died and left Lucille her car. But Jerry didn't give up. Someday she'd see that what she was doing didn't make any sense, that life could be smooth and calm and peaceful if only she'd do what she was supposed to. Meantime he'd have to do what he could.

When he found out that Lucille was hanging around with a young Mexican laborer who worked at the gin, he had the man picked up and deported back to Mexico. When she began to hang around with various other local rakehells, he sat in his office and plotted how to make them go away too. At home he tried his best to remain calm and detached.

But the problems with Lucille were only the beginning. Cracks had begun to appear in the nearly perfect structure he'd built of his life, and once they started they just kept getting worse. On the outside things still looked good. The gin was making money. He'd been elected president of the Chamber of Commerce and vice president of the Optimists and a deacon of the First Baptist Church. Both he and Diane were driving new Cadillacs now. The house had a new central-air-conditioning system that could "freeze the balls off a brass monkey," as the man who'd installed it said. And the weather was no worse than usual, cotton prices were okay. To anyone looking at his life from the outside, things seemed fine: a man approaching forty who had accomplished most of what he thought he was supposed to accomplish and was now reaping the rewards. But Jerry could feel it starting to slip.

Sometimes lately, especially at night, as he sat in front of the TV, he had begun to wonder about things he never thought he'd have to wonder about. First there was Lucille, and then Diane started. It was as if something deep and hidden had come unmoored.

Some of the things he noticed were just details. For instance, one night he'd come in from work and there was a new light fixture in the kitchen—a bowl-shaped one where before there'd been one shaped more like a globe. The pieces of the old one were in the trash. He waited to see what Diane would say about it. Such little things were the main stuff of their conversations. But she never said a word, as if she no longer wanted to talk about things like that.

Not long after, he began to notice she was going out a lot at night. She always said she was going to the grocery store, but it seemed to take her a long time, and most times when she came back she didn't have whatever it was she'd gone after. At first he thought maybe the store was just out of things, but one night she said she was going for eggs and while she was gone he went to the refrigerator and saw seven eggs already there. And after she came back he looked again, and there were still seven eggs.

He tried to remember when she'd first started doing this, but he wasn't sure. He began timing her outings and found out she was always gone about an hour or an hour and a half. One evening he was able to check the mileage on her car. He discovered she'd driven twenty miles. The Piggly Wiggly was only half a mile away, and the Mini Mart was just two miles. Where could she have gone? He watched her carefully, looking for other clues, but there didn't seem to be anything else. She was the same as always, only maybe a little more distracted.

As someone who'd spent his life trying to do the expected thing, Jerry had a hard time imagining what the cause of his wife's behavior could be. Unexpected behavior had always seemed random and incomprehensible to him. He felt like he was trying to guess a roll of the dice. But finally the thought hit him that maybe Diane was having a love affair. The moment this idea entered his mind he tried to put it away, to pretend he hadn't had that thought at all, but it wouldn't go away. He remembered stories he'd heard in the barbershop about certain people, married people even, who had had these things. Diane's sister, Lucinda, had had so many that she was like a local joke, a family embarrassment. She'd finally topped it all by leaving town with a fiddler. Jerry wondered if having affairs was genetic, like hereditary insanity. That would explain Lucille too. Nobody in Jerry's family had ever shown such tendencies. They were all normal.

He spent a lot of time alternately trying to discount this idea and trying to figure out who Diane was seeing. An hour or so three nights a week didn't seem like much time, but, not knowing how these things worked, Jerry decided maybe it was enough. Maybe she was going out during the day too. He took to phoning home at odd times to see if Diane was there. But either the phone was busy or she answered it. Sometimes when she answered, he'd ask her some little question to justify his call, but sometimes he'd just sit there listening to her voice say, "Hello? Hello?" and then hang up. Even though the ginning season was starting and he had a lot of work to do, he found himself more and more distracted, sitting at his desk with his head propped in his hands, thinking about this. He considered asking his office girl, Sharon, what she knew about love affairs, just to get some information, but he decided not to. She might get the wrong idea. How, oh how, he lamented in silence, after living life so carefully, can this be happening to me? He kept imagining Diane in the arms of a man of exactly the type he'd decided at the age of fourteen not to become—somebody wild and unreliable and unshaven. As the giant brick burr burners began sending up their smoke, painting the sunsets fabulous reds and purples, he tormented himself with jealousy and watched his wife the way a gambler who's put all his money on one number watches a spin of the wheel. He took the pistol from the office safe and put it in the glove compartment of his car like a private symbol of his despair.

One evening in the middle of November when the sand was blowing hard, Jerry was sitting in front of the TV as he always did after dinner. It was a Wednesday and Diane had already been out one night this week. The previous week he'd tried to win her back by bringing her a dozen roses he'd driven all the way to Lubbock to pick up, but she'd only asked him what he'd done and eyed him suspiciously. He said *he* hadn't done anything, he'd only brought her roses because she was his wife and a man was allowed to bring his wife roses whenever he wanted to. He'd hoped she'd show guilt or remorse or even coldness, something definite he could fight against, but all she did was put the roses in a vase until they wilted and then throw them out one day when he was at work. His mood sank deeper than ever. Should he confront her? Should he continue as he had and hope it would blow over?

As he sat there in front of the TV he heard Diane moving around in the kitchen behind him. The dishwasher door closed, and it began to make its low chugging. A cupboard opened and closed. Then the refrigerator opened and closed.

"We're about out of syrup and I might want to make

pancakes in the morning," she said, sounding very casual. "I think I'll go pick some up."

Jerry gripped the arms of his chair. "I'll go get it for you," he said. Diane had not made pancakes in five years. She didn't even like pancakes.

"What? No, that's okay," she said, too quickly, he thought. "You just stay there and watch your TV show. I'll go. There's a special kind I want, and you'd just buy Log Cabin."

She was trying to act just like a woman who actually intended to make pancakes.

Jerry stared at the TV without watching it, following Diane around the house with his hearing and his peripheral vision and his anxiety, like an air-traffic controller working in a heavy fog.

"Won't be gone long," she said at the door. "If Bobbi Jo calls, tell her I'll call her back in the morning."

As soon as the door closed, he was out of his chair, peeking through the crack in the curtains with a knot the size of a cantaloupe in his stomach. She pushed through the wind to her car and got in. The headlights came on in the dusk and the car started moving. The phone on the little table beside him began to ring. He glanced at it but did not answer. When Diane had backed out of the driveway and gone down the street a little ways, he flung the front door open and ran out into the yard as if he would run after her. Her car turned at the end of the block. He watched it out of sight, then rushed back and slammed the front door and jumped into his own car and followed. When he turned at the end of the block, he could see her taillights up ahead, and when he saw the brake lights flash, he slowed down, trying to keep an even distance.

Jerry usually talked to himself when he was alone in the car, but now he drove silently. He didn't even think, except about the necessity of not being seen. He was afraid of what might come into his mind if he started thinking, and of what might come out of his mouth if he unclenched his jaw.

The sandstorm had almost completely emptied the streets of traffic. He had to stay way back to be sure he wasn't noticed. The only traffic light in town was green when Diane got to it, and she turned right. By the time Jerry got there it was red, but no one was coming, so he ran it, feeling reckless and desperate. Where the road forked, just past the Dairy Queen, she took the left branch, which ran behind the park, headed out past a few houses, and became the Old Wilson Road.

Here Jerry let her gain a big lead because theirs were the only two cars on the road. Except for a few farmhouses set at the back of big, flat fields there would be nothing until she came to Wilson, thirty miles away. Where could she be going? Nobody used this road anymore, because it didn't go anywhere you couldn't go by some better way. There was no reason to take it unless she was going to one of the farms. He tried to think who owned them. There was old man Kirby's place, but he was nearly seventy-five and his son, who ran it now, was just married. There was the old Godley place. Who was there now? Some guy from Tascosa. Jerry had met him but couldn't remember his name. He remembered him being big though, like an athlete, and wearing a diamond ring with a horseshoe on it on his little finger. He was divorced or something, Jerry'd heard.

Up ahead, Diane's taillights turned, following the bend in the road at the old Merwyn cemetery. A few minutes later she swung around the only other curve in the road. Then, five miles farther on, Jerry saw her brake lights flash as she turned left off the pavement onto a dirt road between two fields.

He watched her Cadillac in profile now and tried to identify the farm where she'd turned. After a minute he recognized it as the Kirby place. He switched off his headlights and turned onto the dirt road to follow. His car bounced in the ruts of hardened mud.

The Kirby farm was a big spread with huge fields of cotton and sorghum and winter wheat, some of them empty now. The distance from the road to the farmhouses—there were two, the old man's and his son's—was half a mile. Way up ahead, at the end of the road, he could see a greenish sodium-vapor light in the farmyard, and below this were little points of light that would be the windows of the two houses. With his car running dark, Jerry had to slow way down, but it didn't matter because Diane had slowed too.

He had no idea which house was the old man's and which was his son's. He'd heard recently that the son—John, was that his name? something like that—was due to become a father soon. He'd be about twenty-seven or twenty-eight, which would make Diane an "older woman."

Her car turned off the road, still a quarter mile from the houses. The headlights showed that she was going down a turn-row between two fields. After a hundred yards or so, the lights stopped and went out. Jerry drove to where the turn-row branched off, then stopped and switched off his engine, and there was only the sound of the wind.

He could see Diane's car clearly even in the dark, because it was a white car and because somewhere up above the blowing sand the moon was in its third quarter. His own car was brown and he was pretty sure she couldn't see him.

For quite a while he sat there in the silence and watched, waiting to see if she would get out or if someone would come from the farmhouse to meet her. Minutes crept by. Nothing happened. If her car door opened he'd see the interior light, but so far there was nothing, just the white Cadillac and the wind and the soft ticking of the clock in the dashboard. He leaned across and opened the glove compartment and groped for the pistol and found it. It seemed unbelievably heavy and very cold and slick, as if it were made of some special metal used only for guns. He laid it in his lap for a minute, then flipped the switch of his interior light so it wouldn't come on when he opened the door. Then he got out.

Moving in a half crouch like a burglar, he walked in a curved path that took him out into the field on the left and eventually would bring him even with Diane's car at an angle where he could see across the front seat. There was no danger of her hearing him over the sixty-mile-an-hour wind, but if she looked out her side window she might see him coming, stooped over, carrying something in one hand.

When he got within thirty yards of her, he stopped. He could make out her silhouette from there. She didn't appear to be doing anything. Her hands, or one of them at least, were on the wheel, and she was leaning forward like a person driving in a heavy rain, straining to see the way. She sat like this for a moment, then she leaned back, still staring straight ahead. Jerry stood there with the wind whipping dust into his eyes until he was satisfied she was alone. Then he went back to his car by the same route he'd come.

In the sudden silence that followed closing the car door he put the gun away and considered what he'd seen. She was driving out into the fields at night and sitting in the dark, alone. That was all. He tried to put this into some context and began thinking about being out here at night. The last time he'd parked a car on a dark turn-row like this was—he searched back through the years until he came up with it—it was with Diane. They'd been dating then. He was eighteen and she was seventeen. They'd come out in his father's old Chevy coupe to be alone and kiss and talk, and she'd brought her flaming batons and twirled them for him in the dark. After that they'd made love for the first time ever, in the backseat with the wind blowing the smells of the fields through the windows. That was the night he'd decided he wanted to marry her, even though he didn't propose for another year. And now, twenty years later, here he was again. This might even be the same spot. If it wasn't, it was a place just like this. Suddenly the intervening years seemed like nothing, as if they were just a dream he'd dreamed as he sat in his car on the turn-row, as if Diane were up there waiting for him in her twirler's costume. He felt like running up and flinging open the door and leaping in and taking her in his arms. His throat tightened with the power of the emotion.

But he didn't do it. He was thirty-nine, and she was about to turn thirty-eight. She had come out here alone for some reason of her own. And he had followed her.

He started his car, backed it out of the turn-row, and headed back the way he'd come. When he got to the road, he switched on his headlights and started home.

⚏ 12 ⚏

Carl Abner McDuffy

Mr. McDuffy had been a schoolteacher from the age of twenty-one, when he'd graduated fifth in his class at Sul Ross State College, up until his recent retirement. His whole life had been lived in semesters and periods and recorded on attendance records and report cards; he *was* Texas History, Room 32, Tyrone High School, just as surely as he was Carl Abner McDuffy. It was all he'd been. He'd missed out on the war because of his eyesight, and there'd never been anything else big enough to take him out of the classroom; he'd never even traveled out of the state of Texas except for one time when he got lost on the roads at night and ended up crossing into New Mexico by accident. So when the time for his retirement came, it was in a way like reaching the end of his time on earth, the end of Texas-History-Room-32 McDuffy. He felt like a mourner at his own funeral. Nostalgia overtook him. Every student, especially the bad ones, suddenly seemed to be an extraordinary being, a creature bathed in the light of his own human sunset. He wanted to put his arms around them, to save them and be saved by them. It was that bad.

For a while he didn't think he would survive it, but he did. The day came and went, and the sun didn't hesitate in the sky, the wind didn't stop; there was no sign of specialness at all, beyond the weirdly naked desk he left behind. Texas-History-Room-32 McDuffy passed quietly away and was reincarnated as just plain Abner McDuffy, an old man. The next week he still woke up at seven, even with the alarm clock turned off. He still sat up in bed and put on his thick glasses, and the room he saw around him was the same one he'd seen for decades. He felt okay. Just the same. If people asked, he said he felt great.

As if to assure himself that he hadn't been transported to another plane of existence, he began taking long walks down past the Dairy Queen and on down the street to Chick Nash Park, where the squirrels lived in the pecan trees and the little memorial to the war dead stood like a marker on a forgotten grave. Everything looked the way it always had, but he felt as if he saw it differently now, like when he had a new prescription in his glasses and things were extra sharp. Sometimes this made him feel giddy and he'd laugh at nothing. Norma would look sharply at him, but then she'd smile. He was okay. He was alive.

So after a while he began to relax. He started taking naps in the afternoons and working on the house in the cool of the mornings, taking care of the things he'd always meant to but had never had time for before. And sometimes he'd bar-b-q a chicken in the evenings. In a spurt of reading he went through two whodunits and two shoot-'em-ups and two historical novels one after the other like a man on an ice-cream binge tearing through three banana splits. Then after three months of this, along about the first of September, he began to dream. He credited it to the combination of pulp fiction and smoke inhalation from the bar-b-q.

The dreams were always the same and started in the fall, the week Norma went back to her job as the school librarian, still two years from retirement. First there was an awareness of a flat horizon covered with stiff grass the color of burlap. Then came the realization that he was traveling across this landscape on horseback. Other men on horseback were all around him. They were wearing armor, Spanish conquistadors. Coronado's expedition! They were on their way to the Seven Cities of Gold, the mythical Cibola. He was a Texas-history teacher brought along as an expert, like a guide to the future. It wasn't an unpleasant dream. It seemed a little strange at first, but that was only because it had been so long since Mr. McDuffy had had any dreams, and he'd forgotten what they were like. And he'd misguessed their cause. They weren't the products of trash novels and bar-b-q smoke. They were the natural outcome of the rhythm of his life. For over forty years he'd spent his autumns lecturing students about the Spanish explorers: Nuñez Cabaza de Vaca, Francisco Coronado, Alonso de Castillo, Friar Marcos de Niza—men with names like phrases of music. But this autumn he had no class to lecture, so at night he lectured himself in sleep talk, searching for Cibola in his dreams.

Coronado rose up in his stirrups and looked across the flat horizon. His golden armor creaked like an unoiled car door. Then he pointed north. McDuffy and the others followed. Two soldiers stopped to drive a wooden stake in the ground to mark the trail.

"Not a stone, not a bit of rising ground, not a tree, not a shrub, nor anything to go by," Mr. McDuffy's mental voice pronounced in his dream, quoting the words of Coronado's report. For forty years he'd quoted that description to his students, and one of them would always repeat it back to him in class or on an exam. They usually intended it as a joke on the dryness of his lectures, but still, they remembered. That was the important thing. After all his years of trying to keep people attached to their own past, another person had been saved from forgetfulness, another marker had been driven into the featureless prairie of memory. In the end it would be all they had—what they remembered. The great goals, the Cities of Gold everyone looked for, never existed, not even for Coronado. There was always the need to remember, to know the past. And this was what had kept Mr. McDuffy going, making him teach hard right up until that last bell rang and it was over and he had to stop.

September came and then October, and November after that; the faint discord of marching-band rehearsals carried in the morning breeze, and autumn and school and time and life went on. According to Norma, the new Texas-history teacher was popular with the students. He was young and crazed with enthusiasm. She said he'd started the year off with a lecture on the Alamo that had sent the boys out looking trembly and overheated and had left some of the girls in tears. Word was he'd come up with a sword from somewhere and had re-created the famous scene of Colonel Travis drawing a line in the dust of the Alamo courtyard and challenging those who were willing to fight to the death to step across it. Jesus, the janitor, said there was a big scratch in the linoleum where he'd done it. Mr. McDuffy frowned when he heard about this, but he didn't say anything. He had always believed in starting the year with the conquistadors, because it related to what the students saw around them every day, the flatness of the plains and the fickleness of the weather. And the conquistadors had been out to explore, not to die. They were following their dreams of wealth, searching for a fabulous city on a river five miles wide where the trees were hung with bells that tinkled in the passing breezes—a Heaven on earth. What they found instead were unmerciful winds and unvarying horizons and hailstorms that broke their crockery and smashed their tents and a sun that cooked them in their armor like biscuits in a Dutch oven. And at the end of it all, nothing: an Indian village built out of mud and inhabited by people who didn't have metal of any kind, much less gold. They strangled their guide for lying to them and then went home to Mexico, following the trail of stakes they'd set up to mark the way.

Mr. McDuffy could see a lot of parallels with the people who lived around Tyrone. Farmers plowed and planted and prayed with visions of Cadillacs cruising in their heads. And then the land beat them again; hail flattened their crops, water tables dropped beyond the reach of their irrigation pumps, the bottom fell out of the sorghum market, it rained during harvest, and at the end of the year they found themselves driving the same old clapped-out pickups, another year older and deeper in debt. Everybody set out in life with high hopes, wearing their personal version of Coronado's golden armor, but most ended up somewhere they never imagined, struggling to make ends meet. It was just like the explorers. Although some of them made it. There was no denying that.

There had been Cabaza de Vaca. His story was like that of the hardscrabble rancher who suddenly discovers his worthless land is floating on a lake of oil. De Vaca had begun his trek across Texas by being shipwrecked at Galveston, and ended up as a deified medicine man followed everywhere by huge crowds of worshipers, lost maybe, but not threatened. He'd heard of the Cities of Gold too, but had no desire to go there. He wanted only to go home. And finally he made it. "I came upon four Christians on horseback," he'd written, "who, seeing me in company with Indians, were greatly startled. They stared at me for quite a while, speechless. So great was their surprise that they could not find words to ask me anything." That was what life was like, Mr. McDuffy thought, not made up so much of the heroic sacrifices of the men at the Alamo as of the hard knocks and crazy luck of the conquistadors. But if the new teacher wanted to start the year with Bowie and Travis and Crockett dying movie-star deaths in a shot-up church, that was his business. He was another generation. Mr. McDuffy knew his role now was confined to that of the old football player sitting in the stands, muttering over the newfangled game plans of the new team but knowing in his heart that he couldn't do any better, not anymore.

* * *

Then one day, as he was reading the editorials in the previous Sunday's *Fort Worth Star-Telegram*, something happened to give him another chance. The phone rang. He answered it and found himself talking to a Mrs. Coleman, who introduced herself as the "presidentress" of the Wilson Local History Club. She said she'd heard that Mr. McDuffy was an expert on the Spanish explorations, and she wondered if he would lecture on the subject at their next meeting. He accepted almost before she could get the words out. He'd be there. Yes, of course he would. Yes. Certainly. Yes. Mrs. Coleman was pleased. The person she'd originally scheduled (Mr. Mertes and his collection of windmill photographs) had canceled (to go to the United Windmill Hobbyists' Convention in Dallas), leaving an unfilled evening. Now the blank space on the calendar was filled.

The Wilson Local History Club had twelve regular members, including Mrs. Coleman, who had been presidentress (her own word, which she always insisted on) for ten years. Under her guidance, the purpose of the club was supposed to be to study the history of the area. Various speakers came to the meetings with collections of arrowheads or fossils or color slides of the ruins of buffalo hunters' dugouts and talked to the assembled members and anybody else who wanted to attend. It wasn't a club of amateur archaeologists or historians, though. Mostly it was just a social club, a chance for a few convivial people to get together one evening a month in the high-school cafeteria and drink coffee and nonalcoholic punch and eat cookies and talk. The lectures weren't demanding or formal. Mr. McDuffy could have talked extemporaneously for fifteen minutes and satisfied them. But he had bigger ideas. This was a chance to speak on the subject closest to his heart, and he had a vision of using it as a launching pad to greater things—lectures to the Rotary

Club, the Optimists, the Jaycees. Maybe even someday a chance to lecture a history class at Texas Tech. He'd show them a lecture! The old athlete would come down from the stands and make plays that would leave the fans gasping.

In this spirit he began to prepare. He had a shelf of much-thumbed books on the conquistadors, and he reread them all, filling a stack of five-by-seven note cards with his small slanted handwriting:

NIZA EXPEDITION (3a)
On March 23, 1539, Friar Marcos de Niza sent his slave, Steven (a Moor), on in advance of the expedition as scout. Steven was illiterate. He would send news of what he found each day by sending back a cross, the size of which would indicate the wealth he had discovered. Four days later (March 27) Steven's messenger returned to the main party with a cross the size of a man. Friar Marcos wept with joy.

Every important event of the explorations found its way into the notes: de Vaca's miraculous removal of an arrowhead from the heart of an Indian brave, his return to Mexico City, the viceroy's vain attempt to persuade him to lead an expedition for the Cities of Gold. Friar Marcos's expedition, Steven's giant cross of good news, the Friar's distant vision of golden walls. Coronado in his gold armor leaving Campostela at the head of three hundred men, their struggle across what they named the Llano Estacado, the bitter disappointment at the end of their search, their retreat across the trackless waste. Coronado thrown from a horse and crippled, finally returning exhausted, a broken man, to die, at the age of forty-four.

Mr. McDuffy wrote and rewrote his notes and rehearsed his lecture to the squirrels in the park. He tried various approaches—amusing, scholarly, anecdotal, homiletic. The squirrels liked them all the same, and the war memorial didn't care one way or the other.

The more he prepared, the more vivid and detailed his dreams became. Sometimes the members of the Wilson Local History Club appeared in them, a hundred middle-aged women riding in prairie schooners like people on a bus tour. They took copious notes whenever he stood up in his stirrups, with the sun glinting on his golden armor, and pointed something out—there, Steven carrying his giant cross; there, de Vaca followed by hordes of devotees; there, stakes marking the trail; and there, on the far horizon, rippling like a mirage, the shining walls of Cibola. Young girl students, stripped to the waist like Tahitian maidens, passed down the aisles of the prairie schooners handing out refreshments.

On the day of the lecture Mr. McDuffy woke earlier than usual. Leaving Norma asleep, he put on his glasses and got dressed quietly and went to the kitchen, where he sat over a cup of coffee and studied his notes for the hundredth time. They were like poetry to him now, or much-loved Bible verses, or snapshots of a new baby. Every date, every name, every word had been memorized, but he still looked at them over and over as if he were a fortune-teller and it was the future and not the past he was reading. Norma woke at her usual time and was startled to find her husband not in bed. She went through the house quickly, not bothering to put on her robe, thinking something must have happened, and was slightly irritated when he nonchalantly offered her a cup of coffee. She went back to the bedroom and dressed and then went to work.

All morning the sky was clear with the hard clarity of the season. In the fields the crops were coming in, leaving exposed earth the color of chili powder where they had been. It was the season of wind, even more so than the rest of the year, and during the afternoon it began to blow. By the time school let out, the wind was hitting sixty to seventy miles an hour. The air had turned gritty and salmon-pink with dust. Small branches snapped off the Chinese elms and flew away horizontally. Somebody said the Mini Mart billboard on the edge of town had blown down again, just like it had ten years ago. Indoors, dust coated every surface. On the six o'clock news the weatherman said it would keep up till midnight.

The lecture was scheduled for eight-thirty. The drive to Wilson only took about thirty-five minutes, but Mr. McDuffy decided to allow extra time so he could take the old, less-direct road. Also, he wanted to get there a little early to meet some of his audience before he started. He'd heard there were people coming from as far away as Neptune and Draw. Norma had asked if he wanted her to come along, but he thought showing up with his wife would be unprofessional, so he'd said there was no need. Now she was glad of it. The wind was howling against the darkening windows, making the panes vibrate as if someone were pounding fists on them.

At twenty minutes before eight, after he'd been dressed in his best suit for an hour, sitting in his chair and crossing and recrossing his legs, he finally decided it was time to leave. He riffled the stack of note cards like a gambler, then put a rubber band around them, rolled up his map, kissed Norma goodbye, and left. The wind slammed the door shut behind him.

There weren't many cars out, and once he turned onto the Old Wilson Road there weren't any at all. It was a narrow two-lane that ran along between big open fields, finding its way to Wilson via an indirect route that went past two almost forgotten town sites—one reduced to only a small weedy cemetery and the other no longer visible at all. Mr. McDuffy took the road for this very reason; it was a piece of the past, and the past was what he loved most.

As he drove, huge clumps of tumbleweeds crossed the road, appearing in the headlights like the wooly ghosts of buffalo. He came to the turn where one of the old town sites had once been—the town of Merwyn, he recalled, once home to a hundred souls. The cemetery was on the left, tall grass around tilted headstones. A dead coyote was hanging on the barbed-wire fence with its front legs splayed out like a crucifixion. Through the blowing dust, he could see plastic flowers, bleached white by the sun, waving stiffly from a Mason jar. It slipped away into the dark. The wind pushed the car back and forth on the road, and Mr. McDuffy had to keep forcing it back where it belonged.

I must be near the other town now, he thought a few minutes later. It had been called "Blanco." *Blanco*, blank, empty. . . . Suddenly there was something ahead of him, two green lights that quickly became eyes surrounded by a shape on the road too close to stop. He swerved the car, but the shape chose to jump in that same direction, and he heard it hit the bumper just as the car crashed over the ditch and slammed into a fence and his head cracked against the steering wheel. A coyote, he thought as he lost consciousness. I wonder . . . how . . . it got off . . . the fence. . . .

When he opened his eyes again, he was blind. He felt the steering wheel. It was sticky. With the habit of a lifetime, he groped around for his glasses but couldn't find them. So he felt along the car door till he found the handle and pushed it open against its bent frame and the wind, and fell out into the dirt, landing on all fours like a dog. His head swam. The earth rocked from side to side beneath him and spun a little. After it settled down, he pushed slowly to his feet and staggered away. The car immediately vanished in myopia and darkness.

After twenty steps, he realized he had no idea where he was going. He turned and walked in another direction for a little way. Then it dawned on him, slowly, hazily, that not only did he not know where he was going, he didn't know where he was. He squinted his eyes and tried to remember. There was a coyote with a giant cross, he recalled. The wind.

It's dark.... I'm lost. And he began to stumble first in one direction, then in another like a horse with the blind staggers, going farther and farther away from the car.

Lost. It's easy to get lost on the Llano Estacado. Cabaza de Vaca was lost for years. Had Indians with him, though, and his medicine. An arrowhead from an Indian's heart. I have nothing, not a stone, not a bit of rising ground, not a tree, not a shrub, nor anything to go by. And blind as a bat.

A tear seeped out of each eye. The blowing dust immediately crusted them to inch-long red streaks on his cheeks.

It could have been ten minutes or it could have been two hours, he had no idea, but for some time he stumbled through the dark and the wind with his hands stuck out ahead of him like a cartoon of a sleepwalker. Then finally he tripped and his fingers found something sharp and springy. It was a loose strand of barbed wire from the fence he'd knocked down. He slid his hands along it until he came to a fence post, which he held on to, feeling over its rough surface as if looking for a keyhole. When he found where the strand of wire led away on the other side of the post, he began to follow it again, sliding his hands along it, cutting his palms on the barbs. Ten yards later he came to another post and stopped, hanging on against the push of the wind and the sag of his own dizziness, but he didn't stop for long. As soon as he could he moved on, still following the barbed wire. When he got to the third post, he hugged it against his chest and let out a high crazy cackle.

After all these years, he thought. It's still here, and I have found it. Only a blind man could have found it. His laughter rose and was blown away in wild hoots as he began following the wire from post to post, not caring that he cut his hands, not caring about the dark or his blindness either, just walking slowly along with the wind behind him, farther out into the fields, farther away from the road, laughing like a madman.

13

Virgil "Bugs" Leonard

There just ain't no tellin' 'bout things. Sometimes life is so dang peculiar you cain't say anything for sure. Just when you think things are goin' along nice an' normal all hell busts loose. If somebody'd o' told me thirty-five years ago that I'd end up workin' on old trucks in a place like Smiley's I'da told them they were a few bricks short of a load. I was gonna be a soldier. I was gonna roll up the Germans like so much tobacco an' smoke them right down to their butts. That was my plan. But here I am, fixin' trucks like it was what I'd been intendin' all along. An' I got no reason to complain. Every step o' how I got here seems like the only one I coulda made at the time. But lookin' back it sure seems funny. Reminds me of a lamp shade I once heard about that was made outa tattooed human skin. That was when I was over in Europe in the Big War. This lamp shade was owned by a German Gestapo officer. I couldn' imagine a lamp shade made outa human skin, but the fella that told me, he'd seen it with his own eyes, an' he said the tattoos looked kinda like rubber stamps. Said one of 'em was a heart with two names on it an' a arrow goin' through. I cain't remember what the names were anymore, foreign anyway, but one of 'em musta been the guy who'd had the tattoo an' the other musta been his girlfriend. It just goes to show how different things can work out from what you think. The guy had that tattoo, he'd prob'ly 'magined showin' it to his girl an' her bein' impressed, an' maybe the two of 'em gettin' married an' on an' on. Or maybe he had somethin' a little less permanent in mind. Heh-heh-heh. But whatever he had in mind, I bet a million bucks it never occurred to him that tattoo would end up on a lamp shade shadin' the eyes of some German Gestapo officer. Just goes to show that you cain't ever tell about things. There's two kinds o' craziness for people to choose from. One is the kind that happens when you think things are happenin' that aren't happenin' atall. An' the other kind is when you think things are all settled an' you don't see that everything is goin' all the time. Sometimes it seems like all there is for a person to do is choose which kinda crazy he wants to go.

It's like this kid works with me. He went off when he was seventeen an' joined the army an' went to V'etnam. Stayed there two years. All the stuff that happened to him while he was over there an' some o' the stuff that happened to him after he got back was so different from what he thought it oughta be that he went around all the time like a man walkin' in his sleep, like a guy I knew in France who got hit on the head with a artillery shell casin' an' couldn't recognize anybody an' thought he was in Buffalo, New York. Ronney, that's the name o' this kid that works with me, didn' think he was in Buffalo, New York, but he couldn't seem to figure how he come to be in Tyrone either. Problem was he'd had all this stuff happen, an' he hadn't been able to make any sense of it. Seemed like it sorta had him blocked up. I tried to get him to talk about it, get it outa his system, but it took a long time. I tell you though, once he finally started he was a real ratchet-jaw, an' what came out was the wildest packa lies I ever heard—stuff about eatin' ears an' gettin' his balls shot off an' jungles with snipers hangin' from the trees like monkeys. I was lookin' for the switch to shut him off after a while. He just kept gettin' stranger an' stranger right up till he got that little girlfriend o' his. Then he began to calm down some. That's what his problem was all along. I wonder if he told her all those stories. Might have. She'd be crazy enough to listen to 'em. She seems like one o' those girls who likes their men dangerous. People like her haven't figured out yet that anybody can be dangerous.

That girl's daddy owns the cotton gin at the other end o' town. Gotta lotta money an' sits behind a desk all day makin' more. She prob'ly thinks he's tame as a old house cat. But I saw him come in here to the station one afternoon, an' while he was payin' for his gas he looked out into the shop where Ronney was workin' on a truck, an' I tell you . . . if looks could kill, Ronney'd o' been blowed all over West Texas by the look that man gave him. It was daggers. Daggers, hell—it was bombs! Ronney talks like a wild man sometime, no question about that, but he's prob'ly not near as dangerous as that girl's very own daddy. Or maybe not. 'Cause, like I said, there just ain't no tellin'. I was goin' to be a soldier, but instead here I am fixin' trucks. Stuff always happens unexpected. Old General Patton wan'ed to go to Berlin, but he never got to. The Russkies beat him to it. On the night o' the big posse old man McDuffy had took off to give a talk to a buncha people over in Wilson an' he never got where he was goin' either. An' that is one o' the funniest stories that ever happen 'round here in my time. I'll tell you how it was:

It was on the night o' the big fall sandstorm an' I was down here workin' the late shift tryin' to get shut of a loada pigs that'd been parked behind the station for a day an' a half on accounta the rig that was haulin' them, prob'ly the world's oldest survivin' Peterbilt, had a busted shift linkage. The fella that was drivin' it, dumb bastard name o' Bumpus, had himself towed in here from a few miles down the road. I knew he was comin' 'cause the tow service radioed an' said so, but I never knew he was bringin' a trailer fulla pigs with him. If I'd o' known that I'd o' told him to go somewhere else. But once he got here there wasn't nothin' I could do but just try to get him back on the road quick as I could.

The job come one mornin'. I called down to San Antone an' had the parts sent up. They didn' come till the bus arrived next afternoon. When they finally came, I decided to stay late an' Ronney an' me worked on it together to get the job done an' that loada porkers moved off.

Now them pigs didn' smell like roses even when they arrived. I had the tow driver put them as far back on the lot away from the buildin' as he could. But you could still smell them. Even Smiley, who smokes those little black cigars that smell like a fire at a dog kennel, thought they was awful ripe. An' by the next day they had gone totally beyond ripe. Nothin' on earth knows how to stink like a pig, an' after spendin' a day sittin' in the sun in that trailer on the backa the lot these particular pigs had become real experts. I tell you, it'd bring tears to your eyes. Turned out this Bumpus fellow had taken the money he had to buy feed for the pigs an' drunk most of it up at that bar out past the Gold Key; then with what he had left he bought some bags o' feed cakes they were sellin' cheap over at the gin 'cause they'd got wet when we had that big rain the month before. Well that feed didn' agree with them pigs' digestion atall, an' by next day the smell was like nothin' on earth. Old Smiley was chokin' an' coughin' like it was a gas attack. Said his sinuses had totally closed down on him. Said that was the problem with gettin' old, that things was always either closin' down or openin' up when you didn' wan' 'em to. Anyway, soon as the bus got in with the parts me an' Ronney got to work fast as we could to get that rig on outa there.

'Long in the middle o' the afternoon the wind, which had

been blowin' steady all mornin', began to pick up, an' by the early evenin' there had come a real sandstorm. Normally a sandstorm is about as welcome as a phone call from the bank, but I was glad to see this one 'cause it helped clear out the pig stink some. We even opened up the garage doors an' the windows in the men's room just to let the wind blow through. Dust settled all over every blessed thing, but it was better than smellin' like a hog corral.

About six Bumpus showed up to see how things was gettin' on. He stood there a while an' watched us while we worked. That's when I found out about him buyin' them spoiled feed cakes. Anyway, we kept workin' away, him watchin', not offerin' to help atall, an' we finally finished 'bout eight o'clock an' backed the rig outa the garage. He went in to settle up with Smiley and had the nerve to ask if he could leave his trailer where it was till the next day so he could go drinkin' an' dancin' again. Smiley told him he wan'ed it moved right then, before the wind died. Bumpus bitched an' moaned some more, but finally he hooked up an' took off.

Soon as those pigs was gone Smiley opened the Coke machine an' took out a couple o' Dr Peppers, an' the three of us were just sittin' there drinkin' 'em, talkin' about how good it was to get rid o' them porkers, when the whole thing about the posse come up.

We were sittin' there talkin', like I said—Ronney was about to take off, an' I was gettin' ready to head home myself but in no hurry 'cause my old woman was outa town visitin' her sister who'd just had a operation over in Waco—when the sheriff come rollin' in lookin' like a man in a hurry. I went out to do his windows an' Smiley went out too, just to say hi, an' while he was tankin' up, he told us about old man McDuffy's car bein' discovered.

It seemed that less'n an hour before, Wintergarten—Ronney's girl's daddy—had called the sheriff an' said he'd been out on the Old Wilson Road an' seen a car piled over in a field, nobody in it. He had the tag number. The sheriff checked the number an' drove out for a look, an' sure enough, it was McDuffy's car. The motor was still warm, even though it'd been switched off, an' the lights had been turned off too. Sheriff said the car had knocked down about twenty yards o' fence. There was blood on the steerin' wheel, an' he found a pair o' big thick glasses like McDuffy's all smashed up on the floor. Soon's he finished tankin' up he went in an' used our phone to call McDuffy's house, which he hadn't done before on account of not wantin' to alarm Miz McDuffy. That's when he found out that the old man had been s'posed to give this talk over in Wilson an' had taken off to go there. It later turned out that the talk had been canceled on accounta the weather, but when they called to tell McDuffy he'd already left.

Anyway, there it was: McDuffy was hurt an' nearly blind an' out in the fields somewhere in the middle o' that sandstorm, an' it dark too, an' the sheriff was goin' to have to form a posse to hunt for him. I said I'd help, an' I volunteered Ronney to come along.

It was miserable when we got to the site o' the wreck. We were out in the middle o' nowhere with open fields all around, an' the sand was even worse'n it had been in town. We parked all three cars—Ronney's an' mine, Wintergarten's, an' the sheriff's cruiser—one behind the other along the bar ditch. There were pink halos around the car headlights when you looked back at 'em, an' we had to pretty near shout to make ourselves heard. Up at the sheriff's car he was tellin' us what to do when Chuck Bonner come up pullin' a horse trailer. We went back to help him unload.

You couldn't see anything in the dark, so everybody had their flashlight on an' there were these four beams dancin' around on the back o' the trailer an' then on the horse's rump when the trailer was opened. When the horse started backin' out, Ronney shined his light in its eye. You cain't do that with those high-strung horses, an' I never saw a animal get so spooked by sucha little thing. It stood right up on its hind legs an' pawed at the air like a rodeo horse. Three flashlights hit the ground like they was dropped in the same move, makin' three little wedges o' light there in the dirt. I hung on to mine, but I jumped back with everybody else 'cept Bonner. All we knew about what was goin' on was the sound o' the hooves strikin' the road an' his voice cussin' an' talkin' to it. Then the hooves stopped an' I thought to shine my light back over, but he yelled, "Don't do that!" Then after a minute he rode over toward us outa the dark, an' in the light that was comin' up from the flashlights on the ground I could see that horse's eye rollin' white an' crazy, an' its mouth open an' slobberin' at the bit. But Bonner was on top now. The others picked up their flashlights soon as the horse was moved away. After that he seemed okay long as nobody shined light in his eyes.

We all went back to the sheriff's car then, four of us walkin' an' Bonner up on that horse, an' the sheriff 'xplained how he wan'ed us to cover the ground, movin' like men huntin' quail, walkin' the field in a row so nothin' would slip between us. Bonner would range on out farther an' see what he could find.

McDuffy's old Dodge was sure smashed up from hittin' them posts. The door of it was standin' open an' I could see the blood on the bent steerin' wheel. It'd already turned brown an' dry. At first we couldn't tell how come he'd jumped his car off the road like that, but after we'd fanned out I heard Ronney yell, an' when I went over to see what he'd found, thinkin' he'd found McDuffy, there was his dog, Mike, all in a heap. You could tell the car had hit him. He was still alive, though. He was one o' those coyote-lookin' dogs, tough as a boot. But you could see he was dyin'. He just laid there with his eyes all round an' black an' his tongue hangin' out with dirt an' blood on it. His side was pumpin' up an' down real quick an' shallow.

Wintergarten came over an' said, "Want me to put him out of his mis'ry?"

"Huh?" says Ronney.

An' then we saw Wintergarten had a pistol with him.

"He's dyin'. You want me to help him off?" he said again.

Ronney looked at him for a minute, then nodded, an' him an' me walked off a little ways an' looked out into the dark. Then there was a bang o' the pistol.

The sheriff, who hadn't seen the dog yet, yelled out an' asked what the shootin' was about. Ronney yelled back, "He was hurt too bad. We just put him out of his mis'ry." An', boy, did the sheriff come runnin' then! All wild eyed an' with his gun out.

"What're you doin' with that pistol anyway?" he said, once he figured out it was only a dog shot.

"Snakes," Wintergarten says, an' he stuck the gun back through his belt where he'd had it.

The four of us fanned out an' began to look again. In our flashlights you could see the dust movin' like a net curtain. The beams were shinin' here an' there out over the field, but there was nothin' but the shadows o' the plow cuts an' some pieces o' dirty cotton caught in stems an' sticks. No body. No tracks we could see. Nothin' unusual.

After a little while the sheriff honked his horn for us all to come back to the car. He had a map laid out with magnets on the hood of his car, an' he 'xplained a new plan.

"That old man hadn' shown up at any o' the hospitals yet, an' I've driven the length o' the road twice already," he yelled over the wind. "We know he's not anywhere close to the car now, so he had to've wandered off into the fields. Remember he cain't see anything, an' from the look o' the car he's had a good whack on the head, so he could be anywhere. Only thing I can guess is that he prob'ly didn' cross the road, so I think we oughta to hunt over that way an' just keep goin' till we find him."

Then he said how he was goin' to check with the farmhouses in case McDuffy had found his way to one o' them, an' Chuck was goin' to take his horse an' go on ahead an' see if he could find somethin', an' the other three of us were supposed to spread out an' move from field to field.

"He could be still wanderin' around, or he could be fallen down somewhere. Maybe he'll see your lights an' come to you."

So we all took off into the wind again. In a couple o' minutes Bonner had ridden clean outa sight an' the sheriff had driven off an' me an' Ronney an' Wintergarten had moved out into the fields an' were just barely in yellin' distance o' one another.

You'd think it wouldn' be so hard to find a man in this country since there's no place to hide. You pretty much gotta be in plain sight unless you dig a hole. But the problem is the fields are so big that tryin' to find a man in them is like tryin' to find a little, tiny screw you've dropped on the floor of a great big garage. An' if you add to this the dark an' the sand an' the fact that the man we were lookin' for was as good as blind an' prob'ly wasn't thinkin' too clear, maybe you can understand the problem.

I hunted along for a while an' 'ventually realized I'd lost contact with the others. Couldn't even see their lights anymore. I knew they were somewhere off to my left, but I didn' know where. Then I saw their lights for a minute, the two o' them together, an' I thought about the way Wintergarten had looked at Ronney that day in the garage, an' how he had a gun with him now for no good reason. Any fool knew there wouldn' be snakes lyin' around out in a plowed field. Snakes got more sense 'n that. I just saw their lights together for a minute, an' then they were gone. I listened to see if I could hear anything, but all there was was the wind.

So I hunted on across that field till I got to the turn-row, an' then I turned an' walked up to the fence on the far side, shinin' my light all around an' callin' out now an' then, even though I don't think anybody coulda heard. Then I came down the fence-row back to the road an' walked up it till I got back to where the cars were parked.

The sheriff was there again. He said nobody at the farms knew anything, an' he was goin' to drive around in his car an' come down a little road that ran along a mile or so away on the other side o' the fields. He told me to stay there with the cars an' keep the headlights on so the others could find their way back, or we'd end up lookin' for alla them. Then he took off, an' I got in the car an' turned on the lights like he said.

I sat there for a while, watchin' out for the others, an' watchin' the sand blow through the headlight beams, but finally I fell asleep.

Mr. McDuffy was the history teacher over at the high school. Or he had been. He retired last year. I guess if a person stands up an' talks about the same thing ever' day for most of his life, it's bound to affect his mind 'ventually. Mr. McDuffy had Spaniards on the brain. One time a few years back he showed up at the school Halloween carnival dressed up in a suit of armor he'd made hisself outa cardboard an' tinfoil. Ever'body thought it was pretty strange, 'cause it was only s'posed to be the kids that dressed up, all except for the cafeteria lady who dressed up like a witch an' served green punch out of a big old pot an' called it witches' brew. But there was Mr. McDuffy, lookin' like Sir Galahad, marchin' up an' down the halls in this homemade suit of armor. The next year I heard he wan'ed to wear it again, but his wife had took it out an' got rid of it before Halloween came. But even without that suit of armor he still was just crazy about them

Spaniards. If you talked to him it didn' matter what you were talkin' about, if you gave him time he'd figure a way to work the conversation around so he could say somethin' about Spaniards. "Yes, it sure is hot. You know when the Spanish explorers came through here, they had plenty of heat, an' them wearin' iron armor too," he might say, an' there you were, back with the Spaniards. If it looked like it was even thinkin' about hailin', he'd start off about how the Spanish explorers had once been caught in a bad hailstorm. Or about how dry things were for them. Or about the buffalo. Or about how they got lost. An' that part, the part about how they got lost, is the important part as far as what happened on the night o' the posse.

Mr. McDuffy had been drivin' down the road that night in the sandstorm. God only knows why he'd decided to drive the back road, but he did, an' there he was, drivin' along it in the dark an' the wind, when suddenly there was Ronney's dog, Mike, standin' in the road. That dog never had much sense, even though he was a good little dog. Or maybe it wadn' the dog's fault. He'd prob'ly walked along that road lotsa times an' never seen a single car. Like I said, nobody used that road for anything except that night, when even before the whole bunch of us went out there both Mr. McDuffy an' Jerry Wintergarten had been out on it. Never did find out what Wintergarten was doin' out there. I asked him, but he acted like he didn' hear me. Makes a man wonder if maybe he's seein' somebody out that way on the sly, don't it? Anyway, Mr. McDuffy was comin' along an' suddenly there was Mike, an' eacha them was as surprised as the other an' they both dodged, but unfortunately they dodged the same direction. The car hit Mike an' then it knocked down six fence posts an' come to rest at the corner of a field belongin' to the old Godley place. When it started hittin' fence posts was when Mr. McDuffy was throwed up into the steerin' wheel an' whacked his head an' his glasses were smashed an' he was knocked out.

Well, between the whack on the head an' the busted glasses, he didn' know sideways from up an' down when he woke up. But he switched off the car an' turned off the lights—God knows why—an' climbed out. If he'da stayed with the car he'da been found by Wintergarten just a few minutes later, but he was too confused to thinka that. So he wandered off in the dark, not able to see to put one foot in front o' the other an' havin' no idea on Earth where he was goin'.

Now I heard all this next part later, an' you gotta remember that this man wadn' in his right mind exactly, an' you also gotta remember that he was a history teacher—otherwise you won't ever believe what happened, even though it's God's truth.

He stumbled around in the dark, goin' the wrong direction from the road, an' finally he ran into a piece o' bob wire from the fence he'd knocked down. When he found this, he followed it till he came to a fence post. Now a fence post is just a fence post an' not somethin' a normal man is likely to mistake for anything else, but Mr. McDuffy, when he got holda that fence post, was convinced that it was one o' the stakes the Spaniard explorers had put up when they was lookin' for the City o' Gold. Which reminds me o' the time a kid from New York who was in France with me in the Big War found a buncha busted milk bottles behind a barn an' started talkin' about how it was a cow's nest. Anyway, he (Mr. McDuffy, not the kid from New York, whose name was, uh, Saperstein, I think) began marchin' along that fence goin' from one post to the next, convinced he was goin' to find either Spaniards or the City o' Gold if he just kept goin'. Problem was he was headed down a fence that led straight away from the road.

No tellin' how far he'd got by the time me an' the posse showed up. He couldn' o' been far away when the sheriff first came by though, an' when Wintergarten first found the car, he musta been almost within shoutin' distance. If Wintergarten hada gone lookin' for him, then he prob'ly woulda found him with no trouble an' this whole thing woulda never happened. But he didn'. Instead he came all the way back to town an' telephoned the sheriff an' then got his gun an' joined the posse, like we was goin' after a desperado instead of a history teacher.

Mr. McDuffy made an awful mess of his hands followin' that fence. He was draggin' his hand on the top wire to get from post to post an' he wadn' payin' any attention to the barbs, so by the time he was found, or found himself, or whatever you wanna say, his hands were almost as much a problem as where he'd busted his head. I guess when you think you're followin' somethin' that dudn' even exist, maybe you just don't take much notice of what *does* exist.

Anyway, he followed that fence line down to the end o' the field an' then went through into the next field an' kept followin' it. At the far side o' that field he went through the fence again, but this time he grabbed on to a different fence on the other side an' took off ninety degrees from the direction where he'd been goin', which is prob'ly how come the sheriff didn' find him when he drove along the next road.

Mr. McDuffy kept walkin' like this, from fence post to fence post an' from field to field, for hours. A couple o' times he stopped an' rested, an' he fell plenty o' times. It musta been an awful experience. But right through it all he believed he was followin' the Spaniards, so he didn't mind. A couple o' times before the dust cleared he even thought he heard the hooves o' their horses, an' right afterwards, when he was still in the hospital, he claimed he'd been given a ride by a Spaniard dressed in gold armor. I guess what he heard coulda been Bonner ridin' by lookin' for him, or it coulda been some cattle stompin' around in the dark, or it coulda been nothin' atall, only his imagination. But crazy or not, I got to give it to him, I never coulda walked the distance he did. Not in the middle o' the night an' blind an' hurt, that's for sure. You wouldn' think a schoolteacher would have it in him.

Just before one o'clock in the mornin' the wind began to drop off an' blow in gusts. By two it had died away an' the stars come out, but the moon had already set an' Mr. McDuffy's eyes wadn' good enough to see the stars, so he still didn' have any idea o' direction other than from followin' the fences. So he just kept marchin' along until 'ventually he began to make out a glow on the horizon and went toward it, sure it was the City o' Gold.

Mosta this time I was asleep back in the car, like I already said. But about midnight the sheriff come back an' woke me up.

"Where's the others?" he says.

"I don' know," I says. "I musta fell asleep. What time is it?"

An' he told me it was after midnight. I got outa the car to take a leak. You could tell by then that the wind was easin', even though it was still blowin' pretty good. A storm like that cain't keep goin' for long, otherwise alla New Mexico would have been blown over on top of us a long time ago.

"Well, dammit," the sheriff says when I got back, "come mornin' I'm prob'ly gonna have to call the crop-dustin' service to go up an' look for the whole mess of 'em."

"Bonner'll make it back okay."

"Yeah, Bonner'll be okay, but I'm not sure Wintergarten could find his way to the bathroom an' back without help. I wouldn' o' brought him except he wan'ed to come," the sheriff said. "How about that boy?"

"Ronney? Oh, Ronney was in V'etnam. He's a little funny, but I don' think he'll get lost."

"Well, if he's not lost, where the hell is he? They been out there for three hours now."

I was thinkin' now about just that: about Ronney bein' out

there with Wintergarten an' Wintergarten havin' a pistol an' all. But I didn' say anything. There wadn' anything that could be done then anyway. So instead I asked, "You think you'll find him?"

"Who? McDuffy? Yeah, I'll find him. Be easy once the sun comes up. Only question is whether we'll be takin' him to the hospital or the morgue after we find him."

We stood there for a few minutes next to the cars. Then I remembered I still had some coffee in my thermos, so I got it an' we both got in his car so he could hear the radio in case somethin' happened, an' we drank the coffee. He had a half-pint o' whiskey in the glove box an' we added a little o' that to the coffee. Then we just sat there an' talked. His radio would crackle ever' now an' then, an' you'd hear somebody talkin' an' somebody else answerin', but other than that there was just us talkin' an' the wind blowin' an' the night goin' by. He told me about some o' the stuff he'd seen since he was sheriff, an' before he was sheriff when he'd been deputy. He had plenty o' stories—lost people, kids mostly, a murder over at a bar in Neptune, a flyin'-saucer report that'd happened right close by where we were sittin' fifteen or twenty years earlier. For a place where nothin' was supposed to ever happen, it sure seemed like there was a lot to tell. But I s'pose, when you look at it right, there's as much happenin' one place as there is any other. It's just that sometimes you don't notice it, an' it takes somethin' like that posse to make you see what's goin' on, that even in modern times you could have him an' me waitin' to hear about four guys runnin' around in the prairie—one with a pistol like a old-time badman, one ridin' a horse an' lookin' for all the world like somethin' from a Randolph Scott movie, one searchin' for cities o' gold an' Spaniards in armor, an' the other one back from the war an' not knowin' *what* the hell he was doin'. An' me an' the sheriff sittin' there listenin' to the wind die an' watchin' the stars come out an' drinkin' lukewarm coffee an' cheap whiskey, an' the radio cracklin' in the background with word of all sorts of other things goin' on out there somewhere that we had nothin' to do with yet. We sat there like that, just talkin' an' listenin', sometimes honkin' the horn in case anybody was close enough to hear, till two-thirty, when the radio came on an' told us about the shootin'.

I only wish I'da been there to see it. It musta been like a skit from one o' those USO shows that used to come around entertainin' the troops when I was over in Europe durin' the war. Old McDuffy had seen a light on the horizon all right, but it sure wadn' the City o' Gold. It was that honky-tonk where the cowboys go—Bigger 'n Dallas they call it. It's got a big neon sign out in the parkin' lot that you can see for a couple o' miles. It was the only thing big enough an' bright enough that a blind man could see, so that's what McDuffy had set his sights for. He finally let go o' the bob wire an' set off cross-country to get there, an' on the way he wandered into the edge of a little playa lake an' got all covered with mud, so by the time he got there he was a total mess, blood on top, mud on bottom, an' crazy all through.

It was about half past two when he got there. The place had closed for the night, an' all the customers had gone home. Just as he was comin' up to it, the light he'd been followin', the big neon sign, was switched off, leavin' him completely in the dark again. But he knew he was close, even though he didn' know what he was close to, an' he kept goin', an' as he come up on the parkin' lot he began to yell out, "Francisco! Francisco Coronado!"

You'da thought he'd be home an' safe now, but the problem was that his craziness had run smack into somebody else's craziness. Old Spud Merton, the guy that runs that honky-tonk, is as crazy as they come. An' he's not just temporary crazy, like Mr. McDuffy was; he's twenty-four-hours-a-day-seven-days-a-week crazy. He never was very normal, but since his wife died several years back he hardly goes out in the daylight anymore, like some sorta Dracula character, an' now he's just totally off his rocker. His skin's gone the color of a dish cloth an' he wears dark glasses like a blind man unless it's night time. I only tell you this so you'll know what sorta guy he is. But maybe the only thing that really matters is that he's been robbed a couple o' times an' is afraid o' gettin' robbed again, so he carries a gun an' once shot a man with it. So here's the problem all in a nutshell: Mr. McDuffy, lookin' like somethin' you wouldn' wanna meet in a dark alley, comes walkin' outa the dark onto that empty parkin' lot yellin' "Francisco Coronado!" at the top of his lungs an' finds old Merton, who's also not playin' with a full deck, just lockin' up the bar an' comin' out with the night's take in one hand an' a loaded pistol in the other.

It woulda been a strange way to die, after walkin' all that way, after survivin' the car crash an' all, to think you finally found what you were lookin' for only to get shot by somebody who was expectin' somethin' else entirely. An' neither what you thought you'd found or what he was expectin' havin' anything to do with what was really goin' on. It woulda been a strange way to die for sure, like gettin' struck by lightnin' or run over by your own car.

But Mr. McDuffy wadn' the only one had seen that light an' headed toward it. Chuck Bonner was out there on his horse searchin' around, an' he had the same idea. He figured McDuffy might be headed that way, an' he was hopin' to catch him. Only he was movin' a little slow an' was comin' from a different direction. So he wasn't quite there when the sign turned off an' he heard Mr. McDuffy start yellin'. He put the spurs to his horse an' got to the edge o' the parkin' lot just in time to see the muzzle flash of old Merton's pistol an' hear the boom, an' across from Merton he could see Mr. McDuffy with his arms out like he was expectin' to hug this Spaniard he thought he'd found.

I cain't even imagine what old Merton musta thought. There he was, comin' out of his place o' business in the middle o' the night, carryin' his money an' all, an' suddenly there's this yellin' an' he turns around an' sees this apparition of mud an' misfortune comin' at him outa the dark. So he panics an' points his pistol an' touches one off. An' just as he does that, from another direction here comes a man on horseback ridin' hell-bent for election right toward him, an' *he's* yellin' too. I bet Merton woulda just asoon gone back in the bar an' started over about then. But you gotta give him credit; he was mighty quick for an old man. There he was with a bona fide cowboy ridin' down on him like John Wayne, an' he still managed to get off another round. An' this time he hit what he was aimin' for. Nailed Chuck just as square as a duck in a shootin' gallery. Knocked him right outa the saddle an' down in the dirt o' the parkin' lot. An' if he hadn' o' recognized him then, which he wouldn' o' been able to do in the dark except that he's got eyes like a cat from never seein' the daylight all those years, he mighta shot him again an' finished him off while he was all sprawled out. But he recognized him 'cause Chuck used to go dancin' there. An' soon as Chuck got his breath back he was able to say what it was he'd been yellin', which was "DON'T SHOOT!!!"

Merton still wadn' clear what was goin' on, but he could tell now it wadn' no robbery. He picked up Chuck an' carried him inside an' stretched him out on the pool table. Mr. McDuffy had quieted right down once there was shots fired. He still didn' have any idea where he was, but he went on in the bar with the other two. Then Merton called the police an' the police got on the radio, an' me an' the sheriff got the message, an' he headed off in a big high-rollin' rush to the scene o' the shootin' an' left me waitin' there where I was in case Ronney an' Wintergarten showed up. I got back in my own car an' turned the lights on an' honked the horn ever' now an' then in case they could hear.

I waited there till dawn, when the sheriff came back for me. Ronney an' Wintergarten had come out on another road a couple hours earlier an' caught a ride into town with a farmer headin' for the gin. Bonner an' Mr. McDuffy had both been taken to the hospital up in Lubbock. An' the sheriff looked about as tired as I felt.

Couple o' days later me an' Ronney drove up to Lubbock to pick up some parts, an' while we were there we went by the hospital to say hi. Chuck an' Mr. McDuffy'd been put in the same room. Mr. McDuffy had stitches on his forehead like a black zipper, an' both of his hands was bandaged up big as boxin' gloves, but he knew who he was an' where he was now, an' his wife had brought him his extra glasses, so he wadn' blind anymore. Chuck had his shoulder all strapped up where he'd got shot, an' he was pretty bruised up from his fall, but the bullet hadn' hit anything that couldn' be fixed, an' he seemed to be in a real good mood. His girlfriend was there with him, an' they were laughin' 'bout what had happened. Old Merton had just left when we got there. He'd come by an' 'pologized again for tryin' to shoot ever'body, an' dropped off a cooler o' catfish fillets for 'em as a kinda get-well present.

Ronney an' me, we wadn' pressed for time, so we sat around an' vis'ted for a while. An' Mr. McDuffy explained how he'd got all the way over to Bigger 'n Dallas, an' how come he'd been yellin' "Coronado, Coronado" when he got there. He got real worked up talkin' about it, like he always does when there's Spaniards involved. His wife kept tryin' to shush him up, but he wan'ed to tell it an' we wan'ed to hear it an' it was a good story.

Few weeks later, after he'd been outa the hospital awhile, I ran into him in the barbershop an' heard him tell the whole thing again, but by then he'd changed it up some an' dropped the part about the Spaniard givin' him a ride on his horse. Prob'ly didn' think people'd believe him. Sort of a shame though, 'cause that'd been one of the best parts o' the story. An' hell, for all anybody knows, it mighta happened. Life can be pretty dang strange, an' like I said earlier, there's just no way o' knowin' *anything* for sure.

R0138410027 humca S T
Tidmore, Kurt, 1950-
Bigger 'n Dallas

R0138410027 humca S T
Houston Public Library
Humanities

8/02 DEC 91